Welcome to Woodland Hills, Colorado

Lassiter Ranch

SAVE THE DATE FOR A COWBOY

A Lassiter Ranch Prequel Novella

Jennie Marts

USA TODAY BESTSELLING AUTHOR

Copyright © 2023 by Jennie Marts

All rights reserved.

No portion of this book may be reproduced in any form without written permission from the publisher or author, except as permitted by U.S. copyright law.

CONTENTS

Dedication		VI
1.	Chapter 1	1
2.	Chapter 2	8
3.	Chapter 3	14
4.	Chapter 4	20
5.	Chapter 5	25
6.	Chapter 6	30
7.	Chapter 7	36
8.	Chapter 8	42
9.	Chapter 9	49
10.	Chapter 10	58
11.	Chapter 11	66
12.	Chapter 12	73
Also By Jennie Marts		90
About the Author		93

This book is dedicated to
everyone who wishes they were brave enough to take a big chance....
I promise you are...

Chapter One

Ford Lassiter sat in his truck, staring across the street at the church wondering again how he'd let himself get talked into this.

He was already late for the rehearsal dinner. Maybe he should just go home. It's not like his presence mattered—he was just the fill-in groomsman anyway.

He peered down at Dixie, the golden retriever who was sprawled across the bench seat, her head resting on his leg. She was the reason he was late. Dang dog had gotten into the trash again and eaten a leftover rotisserie chicken and half a chocolate cake, so he couldn't leave her alone until he knew she was okay. Although, he'd take spending time with his dog over being the last-minute sub at a wedding any day. And if you asked him, dogs—even ornery and injured ones—were still easier than people. His dog would never ask him to pinch-hit for an absent groomsman.

He *had* agreed to do it, though. Of course, he had. He'd grown up with the groom, Brody Tate, and had been happy for the single dad when he'd found Elle Brooks. The guy had been dealt a raw hand when he'd lost his wife six years ago.

"Please Ford," Elle had practically begged when they'd asked him. "It would mean a lot to us. And I promise we won't ask you to do anything extra. Plus, the tux is already paid for."

She knew him too well—appealing to his empathy, his introverted personality, and his frugalness all in one breath.

"Why do you even need me?" he'd asked, still trying to get out of it. "You've already got *six* other guys."

"But I have *seven* bridesmaids," Elle explained. "And I just *can't* make one of them walk down the aisle alone."

"Okay, I get that. But Brody's got a huge extended family." He'd turned to address the groom. "Seems like you can't throw a rock in this county without hitting one of your cousins."

Brody had shrugged. "True. But you're like family to me, too."

How could he say no after a statement like that?

Ford sighed. "I should probably get in there," he told the dog. But he didn't move to get out of the truck. His arm rested on the open window, the warm summer air filling the cab with scents of pine and freshly mown grass. He loved living in the mountains, and summer in Colorado was a mix of hot sunny days and cool nights with star-filled skies.

The door of the church opened, and a tall woman with chestnut-colored hair slipped out then held the door so it would quietly shut behind her. She looked to be about his age, early thirties—probably one of Elle's friends—since he didn't recognize her from being around here. Not that he knew every single person in the small town of Creedence, but he knew most, and she didn't look familiar. Her curly hair was pulled up in some kind of bun/ponytail combination, and she wore a plain sleeveless black dress with flat sandals. She had a large pink tote bag over her shoulder, and something wrapped in a napkin clutched in her hand.

SAVE THE DATE FOR A COWBOY

After looking both directions, she hurried across the sidewalk to the small park next to the church. Sinking onto a bench, she gingerly set her tote on the seat next to her, then unwrapped the napkin and pulled a piece from what looked like a dinner roll. But instead of popping it into her mouth, she dropped it into the tote bag.

What the heck?

Ford tilted his head as he tried to discern what he was seeing. At first, he'd thought she was part of the wedding party, but now he wasn't sure. It was obvious she had snuck out of the church, but had she been in there as a guest, or as a pilfering interloper? Although why would she steal food then *not* eat it?

His eyes narrowed as he watched her have quite an animated conversation with the bag, alternately frowning then smiling as she dropped more chunks of bread into it.

He couldn't take his eyes off her. She was attractive, in that cute way where a woman's smile transformed her face, and he somehow imagined she had a great sense of humor. At least that's how it looked, but he'd have to ask the tote bag to be sure.

There had to be more to what he was seeing—maybe she was talking on the phone or had one of those earbud things in her ear. But it sure looked like she was conversing *with* the bag.

He knew he needed to go inside, to at least make an appearance, but this woman, and her tote bag, had his interest piqued. She laughed, a small laugh, but the sound of it carried through the air, and he caught himself smiling. She had a great laugh.

Then he frowned. *Wait.* Did she somehow imagine that her tote bag was talking back to her?

He took his cowboy hat from the dash and pushed it onto his head before opening the truck door, stepping out and then turning to tell Dixie to stay. But the golden's curiosity must've been piqued as well, because she jumped off the seat and went tearing across the street, running straight for the woman.

"Ah hell," Ford muttered, as he took off after the dog. Dixie came to a stop in front of the bench and held her paw out as if she were introducing herself. The woman laughed again and shook Dixie's paw, which sent the dog into a tizzy of excitement as she tried to sit but could only wiggle her furry butt as her tail wagged about a million miles an hour.

Then the woman cooed something cute to the dog and reached out to ruffle her ears, which was all the encouragement Dixie needed. By the time Ford made it to them, Dixie had jumped onto the bench, lay down and had her head on the woman's thigh.

"Dang, I'm so sorry," Ford said, trying to catch his breath. "She doesn't usually take off on me like that."

"She's adorable," the woman said with another laugh aimed more at the dog's flagrant ploy for attention as Dixie nudged her hand with her nose whenever she stopped petting her. "What's her name?"

"Dixie, mostly. Trouble, occasionally."

The woman peered down at the dog. "Hello Dixie. You don't look like trouble to me."

"And I'm Ford. Lassiter." He didn't know why he made it sound like two first names, or why his mouth had suddenly gone dry, or his hands had started to sweat.

"Nice to meet you. I'm Bit—," she started to say, then stopped and lifted her chin, almost as if in defiance, as she peered up at him. "Elizabeth. I'm Elizabeth Cole."

"I gathered that," he said, nodding to the name tag stuck to the front of her dress.

Her hands fluttered to the tag, and she pressed the edges back down where it had started to pull loose.

Dixie had been sneakily scooting forward, covering more and more of Elizabeth's lap, and also covering her dress in tawny-colored hair, which Ford noticed was a little similar to the color of the woman's hair—layers of blonde and caramel and chestnut swirled throughout her curls. He could now see that her hair had been pulled up but several of the ringlets had come free and curled around her neck.

He pressed his lips together to keep his comment to himself. He'd apparently been spending way too much time at the ranch and conversing mainly with his brothers and his horse, because wow, was he ever out of touch when it came to talking to women. Thank goodness he had *not* just said he thought her hair looked like his dog's.

He swallowed, trying to think of something else to say. "I'm awful sorry about my dog. She's normally pretty friendly, but I've never seen her take to someone like she's doing to you. You can push her down, though. She's getting hair all over your nice dress."

The woman waved away his concerns. "Don't worry about it. I love dogs. And this isn't that nice of a dress. From what one of the other bridesmaids just told me…," she changed her voice to take on a snootier tone, "black is apparently not *appropriate* to wear to a summer wedding."

"Oh, you're one of the bridesmaids."

"One of *seven*. Who needs that big of a bridal party anyway? I offered to drop out when we heard one of the groomsmen had appendicitis and couldn't make it. But apparently, they knew someone who would fit into his tux and talked some poor schmuck into being the last-minute stand-in."

A grin tugged at the corner of his lips.

She tilted her head. "What?"

"You're looking at the poor schmuck."

"Oh no. Oh my gosh. I'm so embarrassed." She tried to bury her face in her hands, but Dixie wouldn't let her. The dog poked her nose between her hands as she tried to lick her face. "I always do that. It's a wonder I have room for my teeth the way I am always shoving my giant foot into my mouth."

"Don't worry about it. I've been friends with Brody since high school, but I had my suspicions about 'the guy that could fit into the tux' thing."

"I'm sure that wasn't the only reason they asked you."

He shrugged. "Doesn't matter. I'm committed now." He glanced over at the church. "Although they might kick me out for being so late to the rehearsal dinner thing."

"They may not have noticed. It's pretty rowdy in there. They set up a pizza and pasta bar with wood-fired pizzas from some local restaurant, and the food's delicious."

"If it's so fun inside, what are you doing out here?"

She leaned back against the seat and let out a sigh. "I needed a breather. I'm not used to being around that many people or having to make small talk. And honestly, I'm not very interesting."

Ford grinned and lifted one shoulder in a shrug. She was pretty interesting to him. He was downright fascinated by her. But he wasn't sure how to say that. "My dog would beg to differ."

Oh, real smooth Lassiter. Why was he acting like such a dork?

A small smile played around Elizabeth's lips then she nodded to the bench beside her. "Oh, she's probably not as interested in me as she is in Thor." She nodded to her tote bag.

Her bag had a name? And it was named after a superhero?

Dang he was really starting to like this woman. Of course, the first woman he had any interest in in years sounded like she just got out of the loony bin.

Although this was a new one for him. He'd never met a woman whose imaginary friend was a giant purse.

Chapter Two

"Thor?" Ford nodded to the tote. "Your purse has a name?"

She barked out a laugh then covered her mouth as if the sound had surprised her. But she couldn't stop giggling. "No, Thor is *not* my purse." She raised an eyebrow at him. "That would be totally weird."

He wisely kept his mouth shut.

"*This* is Thor." She tilted the bag toward him so he could see inside.

A small fluffy orange head popped out of the bag and proceeded to try to lick Elizabeth's chin and sniff Dixie's head at the same time. The dog was about the cutest darn thing he'd ever seen. And Dixie must have agreed, because her tail was going crazy again as it wagged and thumped the bench as she tried to lick the little dog's ears.

The dog scrambled out of the bag and into Elizabeth's lap, and she cuddled it to her chest.

A dog. It all made so much more sense now.

"He's a cute little thing. I don't think I've ever seen one like him."

"He's called a Havanese. I think the breed originally has some bichon, and he may have a little poodle mixed in."

"Sounds fancy."

"Ha. You wouldn't think so if you'd seen him eating the potato peel he dug out of the trash the other day. My neighbor bought him, thinking he would be a toy dog, but he grew into this beast at sixteen pounds, so she gave him to me. Well, she traded him to me for my apartment."

Ford blinked. "You traded that little scrap of a dog for an *apartment*?"

She made a sound like an embarrassed laugh as she shook her head. "It's not like it sounds. We live in the same building, just on different floors, but she really wanted the ground floor apartment instead of her third floor one, so we talked to the landlord and just traded."

"Who got the better end of the deal?" he couldn't help asking.

She shrugged. "She got a walkout terrace and my gorgeous flower garden, and I got a tiny balcony and a bathtub that leaks. But I also got this little cutie, so I think I came out ahead." Cuddling the dog closer, he licked her chin, and she let out another laugh.

Ford's stomach did a weird little somersault, and he found he wanted to make her laugh again. "Who needs to spend time on a flower garden when you could be cleaning up dog poop instead?"

Ugh. Dude. That wasn't even funny.

She offered him a small courtesy laugh anyway.

Time to make his escape before he said something else humiliating. He jerked a thumb at the church. "I'd better get in there. Make an appearance at least." He patted his leg. "Come on, Dixie."

The golden wiggled closer to Elizabeth.

"I'm totally fine if she stays out here with me," she told him.

"Oh no. I couldn't ask you to do that. She can wait in the truck."

"It's no bother. And you're not asking. I'm offering. Besides, with all the enthusiasm you've been showing for the event, I can't imagine you'll be in there long." She grinned, and her eyes sparkled with amusement.

"You sure?" He was torn between not wanting to saddle her with his dog but also hoping to talk to her again.

"I'm positive."

"I shouldn't be more than ten minutes."

"Take twenty." She waved away his concern then stroked a hand over Dixie's neck. "We'll be fine. Now get in there before all the pizza's gone."

"Yes, ma'am." He offered her a grin then told Dixie to stay before hurrying across the sidewalk and up the steps of the church.

He had one seconds pause about leaving his dog with a stranger, but Elizabeth was one of Elle's bridesmaids, and Elle was a great judge of character. And it's not like she was going anywhere. At least not until after the wedding.

And he wasn't really worried about the dog. One of the nice things about living in a small town where everyone knew you was that most of them also knew your dog. Dixie would often sit outside a store or the bank while he ran inside for something. She was friends with half of the town.

And Elizabeth had made a good point, leaving the dog outside gave him a good excuse to get into the rehearsal dinner and get out again.

The sound of laughter and conversation wafted up from the church basement, and the heels of Ford's cowboy boots knocked against the wooden floor as he made his way into the reception area. He'd put on clean jeans and a blue button-up for the occasion but saved his 'church boots' to wear tomorrow.

The buffet table was against the side wall with a bar set up at the end. Elizabeth was right, the pizza did look amazing. He grabbed a plate, filled it with a couple of slices and a spoonful of baked pasta. His stomach growled at the scents of garlic, tomato, and parmesan, and he realized he'd skipped breakfast that morning as he'd been dealing with Dixie.

A gorgeous dark-haired woman in a snug-fitting short dress stepped in line behind him, and she held out her plate next to his as he was scooping up the pasta. "I'll take some of that too, if you don't mind."

"I don't mind at all," he said, filling the spoon then depositing it on her plate next to a slice of cheese pizza.

"Thanks, it smells amazing," she said, inhaling the scent of the pasta. "I just got here, and I'm starving. I'm so glad I didn't miss the food."

"I hear you. I'm late too."

"I think Elle will forgive me as long as I'm on time tomorrow."

"Bridesmaid?"

She nodded. "Groomsman?"

He nodded back.

They'd reached the end of the table, and he picked up two sets of plastic cutlery wrapped in a napkin and passed one to her. He dropped the other in his front pocket then nodded to the bartender. He was one of the owners of the restaurant who had catered the event, and Ford had known him for years. "Hey Mike. How's it going?"

"Can't complain," Mike said, with a shrug. "What can I get you?"

He pointed to one of the microbrews lined up on the side of the bar then turned back to the woman behind him. He didn't think she was from around here—he didn't recognize her at least. "You want something?"

"Glass of white wine would be wonderful."

Ford set down his plate and reached for his wallet.

"Open bar," Mike told him, then nodded to the clear pitcher next to the register. "But tips are appreciated."

Ford dropped a five into the jar before taking the beer. An empty table sat a few steps away, and he dropped into a chair and was halfway through his first slice of pizza when the woman sank into the chair next to him.

"Geez, this place is like a rodeo. Do Brody and Elle know any men who *aren't* cowboys?" she asked as she stabbed a pasta noodle with a plastic fork.

"What do you have against cowboys?"

She shrugged. "Nothing. They're just not really my type." She pointed across the room with a hungry look in her eyes. "Now *that* is my kind of guy. Next round is on me if you can score me an introduction."

Ford followed her line of sight and grinned at the guy wearing glasses and sitting by himself at a table, his concentration laser-focused on the open laptop in front of him. He arched an eyebrow at the woman, trying to decide if she was serious or not. With her gorgeous looks, long blond hair and tan legs, she could be a model. He didn't know a fig about handbags or dresses, but even a hick cowboy like him recognized they were expensive. With the heads she was turning, she could have just about any single guy in the room.

"Are you talking about Liam? The guy with the glasses and his nose stuck in the computer?"

She nodded, waggling her eyebrows. "Oh yeah. Smart guys are hot. They totally turn me on. I love it when they talk *nerdy* to me."

He chuckled. "Okay. That might have been a little too much information for me. But you sure know how to spot 'em. Liam went to high school with us, then left for several years to go to some fancy school out east. He does some kind of computer work for the government, but he came back home last year to help out with his dad's farm. Sorry to break it to you, but he's a cowboy too, albeit a smart one."

As if on cue, Liam snapped the laptop shut and stood, tucking the computer under the arm of his pressed blue oxford shirt. As he headed toward the buffet table, his jeans and cowboy boots came into sight.

"The glasses are so hot, I'll let the boots slide," the woman said, grinning and running her tongue over her top lip as if imagining Liam were a decadent dessert.

Ford chuckled again. This woman was cracking him up. He nodded and extended his hand as the other man started to pass their table. "Hey Liam, good to see you, man."

Liam stopped and smiled as he shook Ford's hand. "Hey, good to see you too. How you been?"

"Doing fine. How was the rehearsal?" Ford hated small talk, and all he really wanted to do was make the introduction then skedaddle out of there.

He shrugged. "Fine. It's more for the bride and groom. The bridal party just has to walk in and then walk out. But there was a little drama over one bridesmaid who was so late she missed the whole rehearsal and so did the poor sucker they talked into taking Greg's spot as a groomsman."

The woman raised her hand and offered him a sheepish grin. "That would be me. I'm the late bridesmaid."

Ford shrugged and raised his hand as well. "And I'm the sucker taking Greg's spot as a groomsman."

Chapter Three

Ford chuckled and had to feel sorry for the guy as pink color bloomed up Liam's neck.

"Ahh man," Liam said, as he pushed his glasses further up his nose. "Sorry. I didn't mean any offense."

"None taken," the woman said, then mouthed 'so cute' to Ford.

"Listen, I gotta go, but I was going to introduce you to..." Ford turned to the woman, realizing he hadn't gotten her name.

"Liz." She held her hand out to Liam then pulled him into the seat next to her when he took it.

"Liz, Liam. Liam, Liz." Ford spotted the groom across the room. "Listen, I need to talk to Brody, but I hate to leave Liz sitting here by herself. You mind keeping her company?" he asked Liam, who was already looking a little dazed by the woman's attention.

"Yes, Liam, please keep me company," Liz practically purred. "Let's get another glass of wine, and you can tell me all about what was so interesting on your laptop that you had to bring it to the rehearsal dinner."

"Oh gosh, it wasn't anything interesting," Liam stammered. "We're just testing some code I wrote, and I needed to check on its progress. I'm sure it would be totally boring to you."

"Not at all," Liz said, leaning toward him. "I'd *love* to hear about the code you wrote."

"I'll catch up with you all later." Ford grinned at Liz as he stood and picked up his empty plate. "Have fun."

He dumped his trash on the way across the room.

"Glad you could make it." Brody clapped Ford on the shoulder.

"Sorry again that I missed rehearsal." He'd texted the groom earlier to tell him about the troubles with his dog.

"That's okay," Brody assured him. "As long as you're here and on time tomorrow."

"I will be. I promise."

"How's Dixie?"

"She's doing better."

"Glad to hear it. She's a good dog." Brody took a swig of the beer he was holding then pointed it at Ford. "I really do appreciate you filling in for Greg. Elle was beside herself when she thought one of her bridesmaids was going to have to walk down the aisle alone."

"It's fine. I'm happy to do it." *Happy to do it* might be stretching the truth a bit, but he was happy for his old friend. He hadn't seen Brody this content in years.

Brody leaned closer and lowered his voice. "Listen, I know I've already asked a lot of you, but I have one more favor to ask. My cousin is in town for the weekend. She's one of the bridesmaids and here on her own too, and Elle is worried she's going to be all by herself and she's hoping you might spend a little time with her. She thinks you guys would really hit it off."

Ford groaned. He'd been here before, and wedding setups never went his way. "Isn't it enough that I'm filling in as a groomsman?"

Was Greg really supposed to be the one who was set up with the cousin? Was he filling in for that too?

"I know. But she's my cousin, and she's a lot of fun, I promise. She broke up with her boyfriend a few months ago, so she's not looking for anything serious. She told me she just wants to have a good time this weekend."

"I don't know," Ford said, thinking about the woman he'd already met in the park. She was someone who he actually *did* want to spend a little time with.

"What do you mean you don't know? Isn't *nothing serious* and *just wants to have a good time* your modus operandi when it comes to dating?"

Ford shrugged. "Yeah, usually." At least it had been the last several years since he'd gotten dumped and sworn off serious relationships forever.

"Just give her a chance. You might actually have some fun this weekend. At least say you'll talk to her. She's a great girl."

"Fine. What's her name?"

"Elizabeth."

"Oh. We've already met. And you're right, she does seem pretty great." He toned it down, not wanting to sound too eager. "I guess I could hang out with her some."

Okay, this wedding setup might actually work out. Although the woman he'd met in the park didn't really match up with the description Brody had just given him.

Elizabeth took turns petting both dogs as she waited outside for the cute cowboy to return. She peered down at the name tag on her chest and let out a small sigh. She wasn't sure why she'd grabbed the one that read 'Elizabeth'. Especially when the tag with *her* name was sitting only a few rows away.

To be fair, Elizabeth *was* her name, just not the one she usually went by. Her parents had wanted to call her Betsy, but when her little brother was small, he'd pronounced it 'Bitsy', and the moniker had stuck. It'd been cute when she was little, not so cute when she became a teenager and developed breasts and curves that were anything but 'bitsy'. Not only had she filled out, she'd grown taller too, dwarfing several of the boys in her grade, turning the nickname into more of a joke than a simple mispronunciation.

Honestly, she'd never felt like a Bitsy, and assumed she'd break away from the name when she went to college. But there had been just enough kids from high school there that she hadn't escaped it. The name had followed her into adulthood when she'd gone to work as the accountant for the family business.

It didn't matter how many times she tried to get her family to call her Elizabeth, or even the original version of Betsy, they never did, insisting it was too confusing since there was already one Elizabeth in the family.

Not that anyone would ever confuse *her* with her cousin, Elizabeth, the aspiring model and actress. Bitsy was tall and considered herself plain and socially awkward, giggling nervously if a boy even looked at her. But her cousin was gorgeous and funny and flirty and could charm the pants off anyone.

She sighed again, and Thor lifted his head to lick her chin. She was just so tired of being Bitsy—that's why she'd grabbed that name tag. She *wanted* to be Elizabeth—not her cousin, she never wanted that kind of a crazy, party all the time, life. But she *was* ready to be her own Elizabeth—to break out of that Bitsy shell and set herself free to be herself.

Plenty of her family were going to be at the wedding tomorrow, heck, the groom was her cousin, too, so she wouldn't be able to completely pull off the name switch. She'd been thinking about switching some other things up with her family as well.

She was tired of working for her parents' business. She wanted something of her own. She'd been thinking about making some changes in her life, too. Didn't know what yet but she knew she wanted to change, *needed* to change—maybe that looked like finding a new job or getting out of that dinky downtown apartment. She wasn't sure yet, but she felt like she was finally ready to take a risk.

Like flirting with a cute cowboy.

A smile tugged at the corners of her lips just thinking about him. Although, she wasn't sure what she'd been doing could be considered flirting, not when they'd talked about her leaky bathtub and cleaning up dog poo.

Dixie suddenly raised her head and let out an excited huff. Elizabeth turned her head toward the church, her pulse already racing in anticipation of seeing the handsome cowboy again.

But it wasn't Ford who had caught Dixie's attention. Elizabeth followed the dog's line of sight and saw a small bunny take off into the bushes. Then the dog leapt off the bench and went tearing after it.

Ford stepped out of the church, balancing two cupcakes on a paper plate. He figured bringing Elizabeth a treat was the least he could do to repay her for watching his dog. He was considering asking her out for a drink, too.

But he froze in his tracks, his heart plummeting, as he looked across the street to the park bench. Elizabeth...*and* his dog...were gone.

Chapter Four

Ford hurried toward the park bench, sure there must be some kind of reasonable explanation. There was no way Brody's cousin had kidnapped his dog. Was there?

"Ford. Over here."

He turned in the direction he heard his name being called from, and his eyes widened as he saw Elizabeth crawling out of a large bush nestled between two pine trees. Her hair was in disarray, and as he hurried toward her, he saw tears shining in dirt-streaked tracks down her cheeks.

"Are you okay?" He crouched down next to her, holding out his free hand to help.

She waved it away, drawing the back of her hand across her cheeks. "Ford. Oh my gosh, I'm so sorry. There was a bunny. And Dixie just tore off. And I tried to catch her. But she's gone."

"Oh shoot. I'm sorry, darlin'. I should have warned you. Dixie loves chasing rabbits."

Her breath hitched as she peered up at him, more tears shining in her eyes. "I'm the one who's sorry. You trusted me with your dog, and now she's gone." Thor was racing around her, then standing on his back legs as he tried to lick the tears from her cheeks.

Still holding the plate of cupcakes in one hand, he used his other to pull her to her feet. Most of her hair had come free from the clip holding it, and a few leaves and pine needles were stuck in the curls. Her chin almost touched her chest, and she looked so sad, he couldn't help but pull her against him in a hug.

"It's okay. I promise," he said into her hair, then he lifted his fingers to his mouth and let out a loud whistle.

The sound of one sharp bark followed by twigs snapping and leaves rustling could be heard right before the golden retriever came crashing through the bushes and sprinted toward Ford. She sat obediently at his feet as Thor raced around her, and the two dogs sniffed at each other as if it had been weeks since they'd been together.

"Oh my gosh. Dixie," Elizabeth cried, crouching down to throw her arms around the dog. "I'm so glad you're all right."

"She's fine," Ford said, realizing for the first time that Elizabeth's dress was split completely up the side and blood was trailing down one skinned knee. "But you're not. You're bleeding."

She stood up, and he reached for her as she swayed a little. "I don't do very well at the sight of blood."

He wasn't doing very well at keeping his mind on her bruised knee when her torn dress was revealing her lush thigh and the side of her black undies. He raised his gaze as he slipped his arm around her waist and helped her to a nearby park bench.

"You have cupcakes," she said, as she sank onto the bench.

"Yeah, I grabbed a couple for us thinking you deserved a treat for watching my dog, but now I realize a cupcake isn't near enough. I'm awful sorry about your knee. And your dress."

"My dress?" She looked down, and her eyes widened as she saw the split going almost all the way up to her waist. "Oh my gosh. My dress."

"I'm a little more concerned with that knee," he said, passing her the plate of cupcakes as he pulled a napkin from his front pocket and dabbed it at her bloody knee.

She took the plate in one hand then reached with the other to try to pull the two sides of her torn dress together. "Oh forget it," she said, giving up on the dress and taking a cupcake from the plate. She peeled back the wrapper and took a bite then winced as Ford wiped more blood and dirt from her knee.

"Sorry," he told her. "We need to get this cleaned up though. Can I help you back inside?"

She shook her head and a leaf fell from her hair. "No way. I'm not going back in there like this." She pointed to the "Creedence Country Inn", the town's local bed and breakfast, located across the street from the church. "I'd rather go back to my room. I'm staying in one of the cottages behind the inn."

"All right. Let's get you over there then. I've got a first aid kit in my truck. We can grab it as we walk by."

"You already brought me the best first aid," she said, popping the rest of the cupcake into her mouth. "Frosting and cake always make everything better." A panicked look filled her eyes as she suddenly looked around her. "My bag. It's gone. I must have lost it when I went running after the dog."

"It's okay. We'll find it," Ford said, pushing up from the bench. "Where else did you go when you were chasing the dog?"

She pointed to the break in the trees to the right of the bushes she'd crawled out of. "I went through those trees. There was a path then she ran off to the left. And it's not just the tote bag. My purse is inside of it too.

I'm such an idiot." She started to get up, but he put a hand gently on her shoulder.

"You stay here. And hey, don't talk like that. It was *my* idiot dog that took off. You were just being sweet trying to catch her." He shot a stern look at Dixie, who lowered her body to the ground then rested her head apologetically on Elizabeth's foot.

Yeah, you better look sorry.

Elizabeth buried her face in her hands.

"Don't worry," he told her, rubbing her shoulder that his hand was apparently still holding onto. "I'll find it." He gave her an encouraging nod then hurried toward the trees. "I'll be right back," he called over his shoulder. "Don't move."

He followed the path for a few steps then could see where the dog, and the woman, had veered off. He tracked their course by the crushed leaves and vegetation and the broken branches they'd left in their wake. It only took him a few minutes to spot the large pink tote nestled amongst the branches of a sage bush.

Gently extricating the bag from the branches of the bush, he took a quick look inside and spotted a small black purse. *Thank goodness.*

Elizabeth was slumped on the bench, both dogs standing sentinel on either side of her, when he came out of the trees and held the bag aloft. "I got it," he called.

She breathed a visible sigh of relief when he handed her the tote. "Oh thank you so much for finding it."

"It was snagged in a sage bush. Looks like your purse is still there."

She pulled out the black purse, unzipped the top then grabbed the wallet and snapped it open. "Everything's still here," she said, clutching the wallet to her chest. "A few years ago, I accidentally left my purse in the bathroom at a restaurant. I realized it within minutes, but by the time I got back, my wallet was gone and whoever took it had already charged two thousand dollars to my card in the time it took me to call the bank. It was such a mess."

"Dang. I can't imagine that happening here. Small towns are different. Last summer, Doc Hunter's wallet fell out of his pocket while he was on a walk. He'd just been to the bank and had taken out six hundred dollars in cash. A couple of teenagers found it, checked the address on his license, and took it to his house. All the money and his credit cards were still inside."

"That's a nice story. That would never happen in my neighborhood."

Ford shrugged. "It worked out well for the kids too. Doc gave them each fifty dollars for returning the wallet." Elizabeth's chin was still tucked into her chest, her eyes cast down. He'd hoped to earn one of her big smiles by finding the bag, but she still seemed upset. He nudged her shoulder as he sat down next to her. "Hey now, darlin', it's okay. We found the bag."

She peered over at him, an embarrassed expression on her face. "It's not that. I mean it *is* that. It's all of this. I came up here this weekend hoping to have the courage to try new things, to step out of my comfort zone, and then I meet this hot guy who seems really nice too. But instead of acting all cool and charming, I lose his dog, split my dress open and flash him my ridiculously dull undies. I'm bruised up and bleeding, and I'm pretty sure I have leaves and possibly a bug in my hair. And that's not even the worst of it." She looked even more miserable as she held up the empty plate. "While you were being so sweet and trekking through the woods trying to find my bag, I accidentally ate your cupcake."

Chapter Five

Ford stared at Elizabeth for a second, trying to process all the words she'd said—he'd gotten a little tripped up thinking about her undies—then he couldn't hold back a grin and a laugh burst from his lips.

Her eyes widened, and he shook his head, still smiling at her. "I do like you, Elizabeth Cole." A small glob of frosting clung to the corner of her lip, and he reached up, cupping her chin then using his thumb to catch the bit of frosting. Then he pulled his thumb back and sucked the frosting into his mouth. "There, now we can say we shared it."

She blinked at him then her lips curved, and she burst out laughing too. "Thank you," she said, when she finally stopped giggling. "You're a good man, Ford."

He shrugged. "Don't let it get around. I've got a reputation to protect."

"As what?"

Geez, why had he said that? She didn't know him. He could have actually let her come to her own conclusions, and maybe she wouldn't have seen him as the grouchy grump his brothers were always accusing him of being.

"My brothers think I'm kind of a grouch." Although, to be fair, he did have reason to be.

"You don't seem grouchy to me."

"Give it time."

She giggled then covered her mouth with her hand. "Sorry, I have an awkward habit of giggling at the most inopportune moments." She peered down into her lap. "And occasionally when I'm in the company of good-looking men." Another small giggle escaped her. It sounded more like a hiccup.

"Good-looking, huh?" Ford nudged her arm. "A minute ago, you called me *hot*."

"Oh gosh, I did." She cringed then buried her face in her hands. "Can you just go back into the church and tell my cousin that I died of embarrassment, so I won't be able to be in the wedding after all. Tell him I'll be escaping out of town within the hour."

"Don't you dare. You're the most interesting person I've met at this shindig, and I'm going to need you to keep me company tomorrow." He stood and held out his hand. "Now, come on, let's go get that knee cleaned up."

Thirty minutes later, Elizabeth came out of the bathroom to find Ford on the floor of her cottage wrestling with the two dogs. She'd changed into a pair of khaki shorts and a light pink tank top. A large Band-Aid covered the space just below one knee, and her cheeks were still warm just thinking about the way Ford's hands had felt as they ran over and around her legs as he'd cleaned and bandaged the scrapes.

"Feel better?" he asked as he played tug of war with Thor and one of his favorite rope toys.

She nodded. "You mean now that I'm not flashing you my boring underwear and a substantial amount of leg."

He peered up at her and offered her a roguish grin. "Oh darlin', a glimpse of leg and underwear is never boring."

A giggle bubbled out of her, and she tried to disguise it as a cough as she planted herself on the arm of the loveseat next to him.

From the way his grin widened, she wasn't fooling him. He leaned back against the side of the bed so he was facing her. "So, what do you want to do now?"

"Oh. Um...well..." She couldn't believe he still wanted to hang out with her. Even after he'd witnessed what a dork she was. *Be cool. Don't act too anxious.* She pushed her hair behind her ear and tried for casual nonchalance. "I don't know."

His brows knit together, and an expression crossed his face that Elizabeth couldn't read. Was it disappointment? The look passed quickly, and he turned his attention back to the dog. "Unless you don't want to. You know, don't want to do anything...with me."

"No. I do. I mean, yes, I do want to do things. With you. I mean...well, not *things* with you. But *some*thing. With you." She stared down into her lap and clapped her hand over her mouth as another giggle threatened to escape. "Oh gosh."

Ford didn't say anything in reply. She was afraid to look at him. With a resigned grimace, she lifted her face, terrified to see the expression on his face, sure it was going to be one of disgust or a look of pathetic sympathy for the ridiculous woman who couldn't talk to a boy without having a giggling fit. Well, not a *boy*, a *man*. Ford was definitely a man, with broad man shoulders and a hard muscled man chest.

She swallowed and met his gaze. But instead of a look of pity, Ford was wearing one of his roguish grins. The ones that made her scraped knees go weak.

"Sooo," he said, his grin widening. "You wanna do *things* with me?"

She grabbed one of the throw pillows from the loveseat and tossed it at him. "You know what I meant."

He caught the pillow and tossed it back to the sofa as Thor tried to chomp down on the corner of it. "Seriously, all kidding aside, I'm game to hang out. What would you like to do?"

"Well," she said, sliding off the arm of the loveseat and sinking onto the cushion. "What *is* there to do around here?" She thought back to the movies and books she'd read with small towns as their settings. "I don't get out of the city much, so I think it would be fun to do something unique to the mountains or to a small town. Do you happen to have an apple-picking festival or a small county fair we could attend?"

He quirked an eyebrow. "We don't live in a Hallmark movie." He frowned. "Although we *do* have a harvest festival in the fall. *And* we also have a county fair. But you'll have to stick around till mid-August if you really want to go to it."

"Hmmm. Tempting, for sure. But I've really just got tonight. What could we do tonight that you can do in a small town in the mountains that you can't do in the city? And that we can bring the dogs along with us?"

"So bowling, rock-climbing, and sky-diving are out."

She laughed. A real laugh, not just a nervous giggle. Under that somewhat gruff exterior, he was funny. "I agree about the bowling, only because Thor can throw a wicked reverse spin, but we might be up for the sky-diving."

He chuckled, and she liked knowing that she could make him laugh. "Can you ride?"

"Ride what? A bike?" she asked. "Like a mountain bike?"

"No. Like a horse."

"Oh. Well, kind of. But not really. Actually—no. I can't."

He grinned. "That's okay. It probably wouldn't work anyway. Dixie could run alongside us, but I'm not sure Thor would appreciate riding in a saddle bag. So, a horseback ride is out too." He drummed his fingers against his leg. "It's kind of boring around here."

"What do you normally do on the weekends?"

"Me? I normally spend most nights at the ranch. There's always something to do, and if I'm inside, I'm usually watching a hockey game or reading a book." He dipped his head and a lock of his dark hair fell across his forehead. He pushed it back. "Apparently I'm kind of boring too."

She huffed. "I doubt that."

"It's true," he muttered. "It's Friday night, so normally I'd suggest going down to The Creed, that's our local restaurant and bar. They usually have live music on the weekends. But we've already eaten, and it wouldn't really be fun for the dogs."

"Is there anything we can do outside? Go for a hike, maybe?"

"It's already starting to get dark, so a hike's probably out, but..." He arched an eyebrow in her direction. "Do you want to get dirty?"

Chapter Six

Elizabeth swallowed and tried to ignore the tendrils of heat coiling in her belly. "Um…"

Ford nudged her foot with his. "I'm just teasing you. But I like where your mind went. What I meant was that we've got a lake, up in the mountains above the ranch. We could go up there and look at the stars. If you want to. I guarantee you don't see the stars in the city the way you do out here in the country. And when you're up in the mountains, the stars are so close, it almost feels like you can reach out and touch them."

Go up into the mountains all alone with some guy she'd just met? That sounded like a terrible idea. Possibly even dangerous. "Sure. That sounds fun."

He was one of her cousin's closest friends, she reminded herself. And she did have pepper spray in her purse.

"You might want to grab some extra clothes. I've got a sweatshirt you can borrow in the truck, but you should bring some pants and a warmer shirt, for when it cools off."

Thirty minutes later, they were bumping along a dirt road as they headed further up into the mountains. Dusk lay heavy in the air, but it was still light enough to see. Ford had driven up this road so many times, he knew every rut and turn by heart.

They had the windows down, and Dixie sniffed the air then let out an excited yip from her spot on the back seat of the king cab. "She knows we're almost there," he told Elizabeth.

"This is quite a ways up into the mountains," she said. Thor stood in her lap, his paws on the door, as he pushed his head out the window. "Not that I'm nervous about driving up to a deserted cabin in the woods with a guy I just met." She gave him a serious look. "I hope you're not an ax-murdering serial killer, because that would be *really* awkward to have two of us in the same truck."

He let loose a loud laugh. "You crack me up. That one was a little dark, but I still liked it."

She laughed with him. "I don't often get accused of being funny."

He gave her a skeptical side eye. "Really? Then whoever you're talking to must not be really listening." His hand rested on the back of the seat, and he caught himself absently playing with one of her curls as he pulled the truck into a clearing between the trees. Then he held his breath as he waited for Elizabeth's reaction.

She leaned forward in the seat, pressing her hand to her chest as she peered through the windshield. Her eyes were wide as she breathed out one word. "Wow."

"I know," he said. He barely knew her, yet he somehow knew she'd love it.

"It's beautiful," she said. "This belongs to you?"

"It's on our property, so it belongs to our family, I guess. But I've never really thought of the lake as ours." He pointed to the small log cabin sitting next to the lake. It was rough-hewn pine and had a small, covered porch that held two rocking chairs and looked out toward the water. "That little cabin is ours though. My grandpa and his brother built it when they were in their twenties. It started out pretty small, just one big room with a bed, a table, and a little kitchen. Then about ten years ago, my grandpa, my brothers and I added on a bedroom and a bathroom with a toilet and shower. And we renovated the kitchen to add running water and put in some appliances so there's a refrigerator and a stove now."

"It's wonderful. How cool that you got to spend your life coming up here."

He nodded as he cut the engine. "Yeah, it is pretty cool. I'm glad you like it."

"I love it," she said, opening the truck door and climbing out. Thor and Dixie scrambled out after her and proceeded to sniff every rock, bush, and tree in the surrounding area.

Ford exited the truck and came to stand beside her, taking in the view as if seeing it for the first time. The lake was small, ringed with tall pine trees, with the side of the mountain climbing up about forty feet along its far side. A creek ran off the top of the ridge, forming a waterfall into the lake. A pine tree with heavy branches protruded over the side from the bank next to the cabin, and a rope swing hung over the water.

Tonight, the water gently lapped at the shore, and he breathed in the scent of pine trees, wildflowers, and the lake. He wasn't sure why, but Ford reached for Elizabeth's hand and entwined their fingers as they both stared out over the water.

He wasn't sure how long they stood like that, could have been a few seconds, or a few minutes, but he would have gladly stood for an hour, the whole night, a week. Something about this woman settled the aggravation and irritation he felt at almost everything these days. He felt easy, content, around her. And that was saying a lot for him.

She turned her head to look at him. "I can't believe I'm saying this, but everything in me wants to jump in that lake and go for a swim."

Ford chuckled. "You'll be in for a surprise if you do."

"Why? Is it freezing? Will I die of hypothermia in two minutes or less?"

He shook his head. "Just the opposite. There're several hot springs in the mountains above the lake that feed into it. The water is actually warm."

"You're kidding?" she said, letting go of his hand and kicking off her sandals. She laughed like a delighted child as she waded into the water. "Oh my gosh. It *is* warm. Not like a hot tub, but more like a heated pool."

"I told you." He nodded at the lake. "You really want to go for a swim?"

She shifted from one foot to the other, and Ford noticed the shiny pink polish on her toes. "Kind of. But I obviously don't have a swimsuit."

"Who needs a suit?" He pulled his t-shirt over his head, yanked off his boots, then shimmied out of his jeans. He'd normally go commando in the water, but he could tell she was already uncomfortable, and he didn't want to make her more so, so he left his boxer briefs on. "I've already seen your underwear," he said, walking past her and wading into the water.

She took a deep breath then looked around the clearing as if to make sure they were really alone. Then she took a few steps back to shore and wiggled out of her shorts, dropping them on the pile of his clothes. Reaching for the hem of her tank top, she hesitated, and he could almost hear her talking herself into it.

He wanted to cheer when she lifted her chin then yanked off the shirt and waded into the water wearing only a black bra and matching undies. Not only because she seemed to have won some inner war with herself, but also because he quite enjoyed the view of the curvy woman in her underwear wading towards him.

She got about waist deep then sank down into the water. "This is amazing," she called out to the sky. "I can't believe I'm doing this," she said as she swam toward him.

"Stop thinking about it, and just enjoy it," he told her, as he backpedaled further into the water.

They swam around for a few minutes then she pointed up at the rope swing. "Does that still work?"

"Sure. You want to try it?"

She shook her head no but then changed the motion to a nod. "Yes, actually I do. Wait, no, I don't. Okay, I do."

He laughed as he climbed out of the water and out onto the thick branch where the rope swing hung. He and his brothers had peeled off the bark and sanded the branch smooth one summer so they wouldn't kill their feet when they climbed out to jump off. He grabbed the rope swing and pulled it toward him. It was basically just a thick rope with several knots tied in it that was secured to a massive tree branch above them. "It's easy. You just grab it, hold on while you swing out, then let go." He demonstrated, swinging out then splashing into the water. He shook the water from his hair when he popped back to the surface. "See? It's fun. You should try it."

Again, he watched her as she appeared to mentally gear herself up then she marched out of the water and out onto the branch. Her whole body was shivering as she grabbed the rope and pulled it to her.

"Just hang on to it, then push off the log and let go. You can do it," he encouraged her.

He watched as she gripped the rope in her hands, trying not to be distracted by the water clinging to her bare skin, or the wet fabric of her bra clinging to her breasts. Trying, and mostly failing.

She let out a shriek as she pushed off the log and sailed into the air.

Then, he watched in astonishment as her legs flailed and her hands slipped from the rope, and she landed in the water with one of the most impressive belly flops he'd seen in a long time.

Chapter Seven

Ford swam toward her as Elizabeth burst up to the surface, arms thrashing as she coughed out lake water. He reached her in four swift strokes and wrapped an arm around her. "It's okay. I've got you."

Her eyes were wide, and her hair was a swirl of curls across her forehead. She tried to catch her breath as she pushed her bangs off her forehead, making her hairdo look even more goofy. But also kind of cute. "I don't think I did that right," she sputtered.

He burst out laughing, hugging her to him. "It all depends on what you were going for. You did it *exactly* right if you were trying for an Olympic medal in the Belly Buster event."

She shook her head. "No, that is *not* what I was going for. I was shooting for fun and sporty—like I had at least an ounce of athletic prowess."

"Well, it was fun...ny," he said, then couldn't hold back another laugh. But he also pulled her closer as he laughed, and he loved the feel of her hand pressed to his chest. "Funny, and also cute."

She splashed at him then did that adorable giggle thing he was realizing she did when she was nervous. Then her giggles turned into laughter. "At least I know all that Olympic training has been worth it."

He let her go, and they laughed and splashed and floated in the lake, enjoying the perfect summer night.

"I think we made a tactical error," Ford told her thirty minutes later when they were finally ready to get out of the water. "I should have brought out some towels from the cabin first. Do you want to wait here while I run in and grab one for you?"

She shook her head. "No way. Swimming in a lake with a big strong cowboy is fun. Swimming in a lake alone in the dark is a classic horror movie scene where the heroine is either dragged under the water by the creepy lagoon monster or dragged *out* of the water by the psychopathic killer. I'd rather freeze and follow you into the cabin."

He grinned. "I'm fascinated by the way your brain works, and I love the way you just seem to say whatever pops into your head." He reached for her and pulled her close again. "But since I am the big strong cowboy in this scenario, I could carry you into the cabin."

"Oh gosh, no," she said, her eyes wide as she pushed away from him. "You're not *that* strong. And having you drop me on the shore would be even more embarrassing than my monumental belly flop."

He narrowed his eyes. "I'm going to try real hard not to be insulted by your lack of faith in my muscles. I'm a rancher. Just last week I carried a half-grown calf who'd cut himself up in some barbed wire all the way in from the west pasture. But suit yourself." He waded out of the water and grabbed their clothes as he headed toward the cabin, stopping to pull the key from where it hung in its hiding spot under the second front porch step.

"I'm going to try real hard not to be insulted that you just compared carrying *me* to carrying a half-grown cow," she called, from somewhere behind him.

He chuckled. "I said *calf*. There's a difference." He turned the key and pushed the door open. "Whoo-ee! It's colder in here than it is outside." He dropped their clothes in a pile on the table then hurried to the bathroom to grab a couple of towels. He tossed one to her as she came through the door, her arms wrapped around herself and her teeth chattering.

She caught it and wrapped it around her body. "Sorry, I'm dripping on the floor. And my feet are muddy so I'm getting the rug dirty."

"Don't worry about it. This is the cabin. You're allowed to get dirty here. I mean get *things* dirty." He offered her a coy grin. "Although you can take it however you want."

She made a sound that might have been a laugh and might have been a hiccup, and his grin widened. It was so fun to tease her.

"You can use the bathroom to change," he told her, pointing to the door behind him. "I'll get a fire started outside. Bring your wet stuff out, and we'll hang it by the fire. It'll dry faster that way."

"Oh, um, okay, I guess," she said, looking everywhere but at him.

"It's okay. I've already seen your underwear. And believe me, you'll be a lot more comfortable putting them back on when they're dry. I'll grab your other clothes from the truck and leave them outside the bathroom door."

"Thank you," she said, hurrying past him.

The dogs had been sleeping on the porch while they swam, and Thor followed her into the bathroom while Dixie ran around the cabin sniffing at the furniture.

He peeled off his boxer briefs, quickly dried his body then pulled on his jeans and t-shirt. His socks and boots were still out in the yard. Leaving the wet towel hanging over the chair, he tried not to think about the naked woman standing on the other side of the door as he headed back outside.

Elizabeth cringed as she looked in the mirror at her crazy wet hair and the black smudges of mascara under her eyes. She towel-dried her hair as best she could then finger-combed it into some sort of submission. Using a clean washcloth and the bar of soap on the sink, she cleaned off the mascara and wished she carried makeup in her purse. Thank goodness it was dark.

And Ford said he was making a fire. Everyone looked good in the firelight, right?

She still couldn't believe she was doing this. She'd actually climbed into a truck with a hot cowboy that she'd *just* met, driven into the mountains, then stripped to her skivvies and gone swimming in a lake with him. Omitting her embarrassing belly buster from her memory, she focused on the times he'd pulled her to him in the water. Her breath hitched just thinking about being pressed up against his wet, hard, muscled chest.

There was a moment when she thought he might kiss her, and if she'd been really brave, she would have leaned into the moment, but instead she'd giggled nervously, splashed him, and swam away. *So uncool.*

But the night was still young. Although she wasn't completely sure Ford was into kissing her. She thought so. He'd invited her to hang out with him, and they seemed to get along so well. Surprisingly well. She couldn't think of another man that she'd so easily fallen into conversations with. But being comfortable around each other, and laughing a lot, didn't mean he was attracted to her.

Although he *had* held her hand.

Just thinking about the way his strong hand had fit perfectly with hers made butterflies take off in her belly.

She needed to get back out there. She'd been in the bathroom forever. She hung the damp towel over the rack and grabbed her wet underthings. She was thankful Ford had suggested she bring warmer clothes. Her sweats and T-shirt felt so warm. She'd taken Ford's advice and was going commando, but the thin cotton of her T-shirt left no hiding the fact she was braless.

It's dark outside, she reminded herself. But she still crossed her arms over her chest as she and Thor stepped outside.

Ford had pulled the rocking chairs out into the yard and put them in front of the firepit where he had a blazing fire going.

"Wow," she said. "That is some fire."

He offered her a manly grunt as he grinned and waved her closer. A silver flask sat on the arm of one of the rockers, and he passed it to her. "Found some Jack in the cabin. Have a swig, if you want. If this fire doesn't warm you up, the whiskey will."

She wasn't much of a drinker, but this weekend was about being brave and trying new things, so she figured it couldn't hurt to take a little sip. She put the flask to her lips and tipped it up. The liquid filled her mouth, and she took a big swallow, then choked on the burn that started in her throat then spread warmth through her chest. "Whoa," she said, around another cough, her eyes tearing up at the whiskey and the smoke of the fire.

"You okay?" he asked, coming around to take the flask from her.

"Yep, I'm good," she said, taking another little sip before passing it back to him. She thought the second sip might go down smoother, but she was wrong, and she blew out a breath and hoped it didn't catch fire.

He chuckled and pushed the flask back in his pocket. "I think I saw some marshmallows inside. Want to roast a few?"

"Yes, that sounds fun."

He went inside, and she noticed that he'd hung his briefs on the side of a large stump next to the fire. Not thrilled with the idea of hanging her plain jane black bra and bikini underwear on a stump for display, she unfolded them from the wad they were bunched into in her hand and shook them out.

Stepping closer to the fire, she gripped one in each hand and held them over the flames, hoping the warm air would start to dry them before Ford came back out. Maybe she could try to get them dry while he was inside. She shook them around while keeping them above the flames.

She was so intent on her task, she didn't hear him come back out until he was right behind her.

"Found some," he said, holding up a bag of marshmallows.

She shrieked and her hand must have dipped just enough for the flame to touch the edge of her bikini panties, because they were suddenly on fire.

She shrieked again as the heat burned the ends of her fingers. Then she dropped her flaming underwear into the fire.

Chapter Eight

Elizabeth couldn't believe it. She stared down at the small scrap of burning fabric that had been her underwear.

Ford put a consoling arm around her shoulders as he peered into the fire. "Ya know, I've been told a guy could light a woman's panties on fire, but I didn't believe it. Until tonight. But I guess it's true."

His shoulders shook as he softly chuckled, and she elbowed his side. "This is not funny."

"It's a little bit funny," he said.

"You're not the one whose undies just caught on fire," she protested, trying to keep the whine out of her voice.

"Well, darlin', I sure don't want you to feel bad about being the only one not wearing any underwear tonight." He let her go and grabbed his boxer briefs off the stump and threw them into the fire on top of hers. Then he held up the bag in his hand. "Marshmallow?"

Her mouth dropped open, and she stared at him then glanced into the fire then back at him. Then she burst out laughing. He joined her and they were both cracking up, the uncontrollable, holding her stomach, occasionally snorting kind of laughter. And it felt so dang good.

When their laughter finally died down, she held out her hand and he handed her the bag. She pulled a marshmallow from it and stuffed it straight into her mouth.

"I was looking at my phone earlier and read that there's supposed to be a meteor shower tonight," Ford told her as he took another marshmallow out, put it on the end of a stick, and passed it to her.

"Like meteors falling from the sky?"

"Sort of. More like falling *across* the sky. Haven't you ever seen a meteor shower before?"

She shook her head as she held the marshmallow close to a smoldering log. "No. Never."

"You're in for a treat then. But it doesn't really start going until close to midnight."

"Guess we'll just have to hang out until midnight then."

He grinned at her, and her insides went as melty as her roasting marshmallow. "I was hoping you'd say that."

Two hours later, Elizabeth found herself lying in the back of Ford's pickup, snuggled against the handsome cowboy's side.

They'd spent the last few hours sitting next to each other by the fire, talking and laughing while they roasted more marshmallows and washed them down with swigs of whiskey. Then they'd grabbed blankets, sleeping bags, and pillows from inside the cabin and piled them into the bed of the pickup to create the perfect setting for stargazing.

Ford had lied down first then held his arm out across the pillows and without stopping to second-guess or talk herself out of it, she lay down next to him and curled against his side. At this point, she didn't even care about the meteor shower, all she could think about was what an amazing night they'd had and how good it felt to be in Ford's arms.

"Hey, you're not falling asleep, are you?" he asked, nudging her shoulder.

She was falling, all right. But it wasn't asleep.

"No, I'm awake," she assured him.

"Good, because you don't want to miss this. You ever see a shooting star?"

She shook her head. "No, not that I remember."

A smile spread across his face, and he pointed above the lake. "You'll remember this. It might take a while but keep your eyes fixed on the sky."

As she turned her face up, she caught sight of a spot of light shooting across the sky. "I saw one," she said, pointing toward it, then gasping as another star shot through the dark. "There's another one. And another one."

"I told you. Sometimes you'll see a bunch at once then sometimes you have to wait five or ten minutes before you'll see another one."

"That was so cool. I'll wait all night."

As they lay there, they saw several more and Elizabeth gasped every time. She'd never seen anything like it. "The sky is so vast. I've never seen so many stars," she told him during a break in the meteor shower.

"Kind of makes you feel small, doesn't it?"

"No. Not me. It gives me hope."

"Hope?"

"Yes. Seeing this vast array of stars makes me realize there's so much more out there than my small world." She kept her gaze focused on the stars, but her voice grew softer. "I've spent so much of my life living in this small, safe bubble, going to college in-state, working for my family, living in a dinky apartment. But lately I've been feeling like I want more."

"More?"

"Yeah. More space. More freedom. An actual house with a yard for Thor. A new job, something that's all mine."

"So why don't you do it?"

She lifted her shoulders in a small shrug. "I don't know. I'm scared I guess."

"Scared of what?"

"Making the wrong choice. Screwing everything up. Failing."

"What are you going to screw up? You get a house you don't like, you move to a different one. You hate your new job, you find another one. *But* you might also find that you love living in a house with a yard, and you might enjoy the heck out of a new job. How will you ever know if you don't try? I think the most successful people aren't the ones who just got it right their first time out of the gate. The most successful ones are the ones who try and fail and aren't afraid to get back on the horse and try again."

She turned her face to him, a grin tugging at the corners of your lips. "Those are a lot of cowboy metaphors, but I kind of liked them."

He chuckled, and she felt the rumble of it in her chest. He turned onto his side and brushed a loose curl of her hair from her forehead. "Okay, here's a non-cowboy analogy. There's a big world out there, and the only way you're going to know if you can fly is to step out of the nest."

She snuggled in closer to him. "But the nest is so warm and cozy. And safe."

"You can always come back to the nest. Or find a new nest that's all yours. And even better than the old one."

"Find a new nest? That's what I've been trying to work up the courage to do. But what if I try to fly and I fall instead?"

"What if you do?"

What *if* she fell? She swallowed, unable to speak as she looked into the depths of his blue eyes. What if she'd already fallen?

No. That was crazy. She'd known him less than a day. But there was something here, something worth stepping out of her safe nest for.

Ford picked up her hand and twined her fingers with his. "Have you ever seen a bird fall out of the sky?"

She shook her head. "No."

"That's because they just keep flapping their wings until they soar."

She blinked back tears, his words touching her heart. It's not that it was the most remarkable analogy she'd ever heard, it was more that it felt like it was spoken just for her and her situation. She wanted to fly…to soar.

His brow furrowed. "Hey now. I didn't mean to make you cry."

"I'm not crying. I mean, I'm sort of crying, but these are good tears." She lifted her chin and offered him a smile. "You're right. There *are* so many new things out there for me to explore, so many new adventures. I just have to find the courage to try. I have to figure out how to be brave enough to take that first leap out of the nest."

"Don't make it such a huge leap. Just try *one* brave thing. Then another. And another."

She blew out a shaky breath. "You make it sound so easy. But I don't even know where to start?"

"Just think of one thing you could never imagine yourself doing. And then just do it."

She stared at him, pulling her bottom lip under her top teeth. She knew one thing right now that she could never imagine herself doing.

Just do it.

She pulled in a deep breath and then reached for the front of his shirt. Fisting his T-shirt in her hand, she pulled him to her and kissed him. It started out soft, just one gentle graze of their lips, then another, and another. Then the kiss deepened, and he pulled her tighter against him, kissing her back, matching her desire with a hungry need of his own.

When he finally drew back, his breath was ragged, and his lips were wearing one of his roguish grins. "See. That wasn't so hard."

"It was for me," she answered, her heart pounding so hard, she was surprised he couldn't feel the hammer of it against his chest. "I've never been the one to initiate a kiss. Like *ever*."

"Maybe you should have been. Because you're damn good at it."

Heat warmed her cheeks, and she covered her face with her free hand.

He gently drew her hand away and kissed her again, softly, tenderly, each touch of his lips sending tendrils of desire surging through her body. Cupping her face, he kissed one corner of her lips then the side of her jaw then skimmed his mouth over her skin as he kissed along her neck. His breath was warm against her ear, his voice low and seductive. "Don't stop now. I'd say your first step was a smashing success. So, what brave thing do you want to try next?"

She rolled over on top of him, sitting up as she straddled his waist. Offering him a flirty grin, she pulled her shirt over her head and tossed it down next to him. She laughed as his eyes widened then a thrill shot through her as his ravenous gaze traveled over her lush body.

The night air was cool against her heated skin, and she'd never felt so free.

Another meteor shot through the sky above them as she wiggled against him then leaned down to speak close to his ear. "Now what were you saying about something being hard?"

Chapter Nine

Elizabeth squinted against the bright sun, shielding her eyes as she groggily tried to wake up. Her head was pounding, and her muscles were sore. Why was her bed so hard? And why was she naked?

Her eyes shot open, and she pulled the blanket up to her chin. A ridiculously hot, and also naked, cowboy was curled around her, one arm across her stomach and his hand cupping her breast like a basketball. Thor and Dixie were cuddled together, curled up by their feet.

They must have fallen asleep last night after…a grin curved her lips. After the best night of her life. Apparently roasted marshmallows, whiskey, and a meteor shower lessened her inhibitions, because she had never acted with as much reckless abandon in bed, or in this case, the bed of a pickup, before.

She'd also never been with a man like Ford before. He was so strong, and sweet, and sexy as all hell. Warmth heated her cheeks, and her body tingled as she remembered that thing he'd done with his tongue.

"Mornin' Beautiful," he said, snuggling his chin into her shoulder, the scrape of his whiskered chin reminding her of the rasp of his jaw against the tender skin of her inner thigh.

"Hi," was all she managed to reply, suddenly feeling shy again. Her hair had to be a tangled mess, and there was no golden firelight glowing over her pale skin.

"Hi," he said, his voice still sleepy and oh, so sexy as he pressed a kiss to the side of her neck. "What time is it?"

"Don't know and I don't care," she said, but her gaze still flicked to the watch on his wrist. "Oh shit. I do care. Oh my gosh. Is it really eight o'clock?"

He sat up, scrubbing his hand through his hair as he checked the time. "It's about five after. Why?"

"I was supposed to be at the salon at eight," she said, forcing herself not to get distracted by the sight of his broad shoulders and muscular chest or the fact that he was *naked*, as she hunted through the pillows and blankets for her clothes. "The bridesmaids are all getting their hair and makeup done today. Oh my gosh. I'm going to be so late. Elle is going to kill me. I'm supposed to be picking up the bagels and coffee from Perk Up. I only had one job, and now I've totally screwed that up. Where the hell are my pants?"

Ford took her hands in his and held them tight. "Hey, it's okay. We can be out of here in five minutes, and I'll haul ass to get you to the salon. You get dressed, and I'll take care of the dogs and make sure the fire is out. Elle will understand." He let go of her hands and reached into the blankets next to him, coming up with her yoga pants.

She grabbed the pants and her shirt, then keeping the blanket wrapped around her, she slid out of the truck bed and hurried into the cabin. She let out a horrified groan at her reflection in the bathroom mirror. Her hair looked like she'd combed it with an electric mixer. There was nothing to do about it now though. She splashed water on her face and used her finger to scrub her teeth with some toothpaste she found in a drawer.

By the time she got dressed and came out of the bathroom a few minutes later, Ford already had his boots on and was waiting by the door. He looked rugged and handsome, and his cowboy hat covered up any trace of bedhead. Maybe she should ask to borrow it.

"Dogs are already in the truck," he said, holding up a navy Carhartt hoodie and her sandals. "This will keep you warm, at least."

She shrugged into the jacket and shoved her feet into the shoes. The jacket *was* warm. And smelled like Ford—like a heady mix of his cologne, leather, and pine.

He'd tossed all the blankets and pillows into a pile on the sofa, and he locked the door behind them as they ran toward the truck.

True to his word, his did haul ass to the salon, but they still arrived almost thirty minutes late. "Thanks for everything," she said, wanting to kiss him, to tell him what an amazing night she'd had, but knowing she had to get inside. She grabbed the tote bag with Thor securely tucked inside and pushed out of the truck. "I'll see you at the wedding."

She almost tripped on the curb as she raced toward the salon and threw the door open. The room was packed with women, not only the bridesmaids but also the mothers of the wedding couple and several hairdressers. They hadn't even started on their hair and makeup, but they all already looked gorgeous. Not one of them was wearing sweats or a too-big hoodie from the back seat of a rancher's pickup.

"Bitsy!"

She heard her name shouted from across the room and wanted to cry as her gorgeous cousin came running toward her, arms outstretched and a huge smile on her face. The real Elizabeth swept her into a huge hug, and Bitsy wanted to fall apart, weeping into her cousin's arm.

"Hi Liz," she said, sucking in a breath as she tried to pull herself together.

"My gosh, what happened to you? You're never late. I was worried about you." Liz wrinkled her perfectly pert nose. "Whose jacket is this? Where were you? And why do you smell like a campfire mixed with a wet dog?"

Oh gosh. With all the racing around, she'd forgotten to come up with a viable excuse for her tardiness. "Because I *was* camping. In the mountains. And I accidentally overslept." That story was at least partly true.

Her cousin studied her as if she were a specimen under a microscope. "You? Camping? All alone?"

"What? I can do things on my own." She raised her chin and pushed her shoulders back, and the hoodie gapped open in the front.

Liz quirked an eyebrow and gave her a knowing grin. She leaned closer and lowered her voice. "I want to hear all about this camping trip later. Seems like it was worth it if you showed up here half an hour late and not wearing underwear *or* a bra."

"What? How do you...?" she stammered.

Liz glanced down as she shook her head. "Yoga pants give everything away."

"Bitsy, you made it," Elle said, thankfully interrupting them and sparing Elizabeth from having to come up with another lame excuse for why she was missing her undergarments. "You're never late. Are you okay?"

"Yes, I'm fine. I'm so sorry. I overslept, so I wasn't thinking about how I was dressed. I was so focused on getting here," she told the bride. Then she gasped as her heart sank further. "Oh no. I just realized I forgot the bagels." Her shoulders sagged. "I messed everything up."

"It's fine," Elle said, pulling her in for a hug. "Don't worry about it. I'll send someone over to pick them up. And you're fine. These things happen. There are so many of us getting our hair and makeup done this morning, you're not even on the schedule for at least another hour. Take a breath.

You have plenty of time. In fact, why don't you run back to the cottage, grab a shower, and change clothes. I promise you'll feel better."

"Yes, okay," Elizabeth said. "I'll be back in half an hour. I promise." *And I won't smell like a campfire mixed with a wet dog.*

"Do you want me to come with you?" Liz asked.

"No, I'm good. You stay and have fun." She backed out the door, forcing herself to hold it together until she'd walked a few steps down the sidewalk and was out of sight of the salon windows. Then she turned toward the window of the neighboring shop, leaning her forehead on the cool glass and let out a sob.

The group of women in the beauty shop—they all seemed so put together and not one of them looked like she had to bolster her courage just to step out the door in the morning. Elizabeth's shoulders shook, and she buried her face in her hands. All her bravado from the day before now seemed like a joke. The things that had happened the night before and all her newfound courage felt like a dream, suddenly so far away.

She'd forgotten the bagels and coffee—her *one* job at the wedding. She'd embarrassed herself by showing up late and dressed the way she was. She looked like an idiot, dirt on her face and clothes, her hair a mess. This was what she got for trying new adventures, for stepping out of her box. She'd put her own needs first, thinking only of herself and what was good for her, but she'd let everyone else down. Is this what she would do to her parents by leaving her job? By moving away?

Pull it together, girl.

She sucked in a shaky breath, swallowing back the emotion. This was Elle's wedding, not Bitsy's Pity Party. Wiping the tears from her face, she took a step back and looked at the business in front of her, thankful the shop was closed. It was a real estate agency, and the window was covered with flyers of local homes for rent and sale.

She stared at the flyer in front of her, the one she'd been leaning her head against. It was for a property for sale in Woodland Hills, the next town over from Creedence. The picture showed the most idyllic little two-story farmhouse, with dormer windows and a wraparound porch. Colorful flowers exploded out of sweet window boxes and a white picket fence surrounded the yard. A small red barn sat across from the house, and a brown horse stood in the corral affixed to the barn. It was utterly perfect.

Elizabeth stared at the window and wished with everything in her that she could jump into that picture, like Mary Poppins leapt into a street painting. She wanted to sit on that front porch with Thor and a glass of lemonade, the summer breeze ruffling her hair as she listened to the low mournful moos of her cows.

The idea of it made her want to cry harder. She didn't have any cows. And she didn't really even like lemonade. It was all just a fantasy. As much as her heart desired a life in that house, she'd never live in a place like that. Although noting the price, it *was* something she could afford.

The truth was, she'd never leave her apartment, never leave her parent's business. Turning away from the window, she wanted to cry again as she saw Ford's truck pulling up in front of her and he got out carrying a bakery box and a carton of coffee.

"I got the bagels. They were under Elle's name," he said, holding up the box.

"Wow. I don't know what to say. This is just so nice," she said, trying not to cry again.

"Hey now. It's okay," he said, trying to juggle the coffee and bagels into one hand so he could give her a hug.

"Thank you," she said, taking the bakery box and leaning into him. "Elle told me I have at least an hour before I get my hair and makeup done, so I'm running back to the cottage to take a shower and change clothes."

"How about I wait while you run this stuff inside then I'll give you a ride to the cottage?"

"No, really. You don't have to. You've already done so much."

He frowned. "What? I picked up a few pastries. No big deal." He jerked his thumb toward his rig. "And you might change your mind about accepting that ride when you hear that I have a caramel latte in the cup holder of my truck with your name on."

She grinned. She couldn't help it. He was just too dang…*everything*. She took the carton of coffee. "I'll be right out."

Later that afternoon, Ford walked toward the barn at Brody's ranch where he thought he'd seen Elizabeth heading.

After he'd dropped her at the cottage, he'd headed back to his family's ranch in Woodland Hills and spent most of the morning doing chores, feeding cows, grooming a couple of the horses, and repairing a broken stall gate. He'd offered to stay and wait for Elizabeth, had even offered to watch Thor while she was at the salon, but she declined both offers, and told him she'd see him that afternoon at the wedding.

He'd grabbed a quick lunch then showered and changed into the gray tuxedo and navy vest and tie that had been delivered to the ranch the day before. Then he'd headed back to Creedence for the pictures. Even though they were in a few photos together, the photographer kept them on such a strict schedule that he hadn't much of a chance to talk to Elizabeth.

The wedding was due to start in thirty minutes, and he'd stepped outside for a breath of air when he thought he saw Elizabeth hurrying around the side of the barn. He assumed she was giving Thor a break before the wedding started. He headed that way and almost ran into her as she came barreling back around the corner.

"Whoa there," he said, reaching for her elbows to steady her as she nearly plowed into him.

She wore a flowy pale pink dress that hung almost to the ground and strappy silver sandals with a small heel. The dress was strapless with thin sleeves that somehow clung to her bare shoulders, leaving Ford wondering both what was holding the dress up and imagining pulling it the rest of the way down. With her hair pulled up into some sort of fancy up-do, there was just too much gorgeous skin on display, and it was taking everything in him not to dip his head and press his lips to the exposed curve of her neck. Her perfume swirled around them, something floral with a hint of vanilla, and he wanted to inhale her.

"Ford. Hi." Her hand went to the side of her hair where she tucked a loose curl behind her ear. "What are you doing out here?"

"Looking for you." He said the first thing that popped into his mouth, then realized that it sounded kind of stalkerish. "I mean, I just wanted to check in with you, see how this morning went and all. Although, it must have gone pretty well, because you look gorgeous."

A pink blush colored her cheeks. "Oh, thank you. You look gorgeous too."

They stared at each other, apparently neither of them knowing what to say next. He wasn't interested in saying anything. All he wanted to do was kiss her again. She had rocked his world the night before. And not just the naked part. Although that part had been pretty world-rocking too. But the time they'd spent together and how much fun they'd had hanging out was what had surprised him the most.

It had been a long time since he'd felt so relaxed and had so much fun with a woman. He liked Elizabeth, *really* liked her.

He knew it was stupid. Brody had already told him that she'd just broken up with her boyfriend and that she wasn't interested in anything other than having a good time. And make no mistake, they'd had a *good* time, but he wanted more. He wanted to see her again, spend more time with her. He just didn't know how to tell her that without sounding like an idiot.

They were both saved from having to say anything by the interruption of the small barn door swinging open near them and Brody's ten-year-old daughter, Mandy, came rushing out.

She looked wildly around then called out as she spotted them. "I need help."

Chapter Ten

Ford let go of Elizabeth's arms and hurried toward the girl. "What's wrong? Are you hurt?"

Mandy shook her head, but her eyes pooled with tears. "No, but I'm going to be. My dad is going to kill me when he finds out what I did. Well, *I* didn't do it, but it's *my* fault."

"Slow down, honey," Elizabeth told her. "Tell us what's going on."

Mandy waved them inside. "It's probably better if I just show you."

The wedding was going to be held outside in the meadow, but the reception was to be held here, and the interior of the barn was decked out in twinkle lights and pine garland. A stage for the band was set off to one side with a small dance floor in front of it, and long tables ready for the buffet lined the other. Round tables covered in white linen cloths with lanterns and wildflower centerpieces were arranged in the center. Mandy led them down the side of the room to one corner where a three-tier white wedding cake was set up. It was decorated with pink and white roses, both real and artfully sculpted ones made with sugar and frosting, and assembled on a table, surrounded by more flowers and what looked like about a hundred cupcakes.

A brown mini horse wearing what looked like a tuxedo vest and an ashamed expression stood tied to one of the chairs.

"I just came in for a second. I was taking Shamus for one last walk before the wedding. I'm the flower girl, and he's the ringbearer," she explained, gesturing to the horse. "And I just came in for a second. I wanted to see it all decorated. And Shamus is a really good horse, *normally*." She paused to give the horse a stern look then peered back up at them. "I know he didn't mean to do it, but…" She pointed to the cake table.

Ford and Elizabeth stepped closer to the table, and she let out a gasp as they both saw the cause of Mandy's alarm. A large horse's-mouth size chunk appeared to be missing from the edge of the bottom layer.

"I know," Mandy wailed. "This is bad, right? I mean *real* bad. He only took one bite, but I don't know what to do."

"It's okay. We can fix this," Elizabeth told the girl as she set the pink tote bag on a chair next to her. "Ford, I need you to grab me some plastic cutlery from the buffet table, and Mandy, I need you to watch Thor." At the mention of his name, the little dog popped his head up over the edge of the bag and tried to give Mandy's chin a lick.

Ford checked his watch as he raced to the buffet table and back. "We've only got a few minutes. We're supposed to be getting ready to line up."

"This will just take me a minute," Elizabeth said, unwrapping the plastic cutlery Ford handed her. Using the knife, she neatly cut off the section with the bite out of it. Then she took several of the cupcakes and scooped the frosting off the top of them and used it to cover the newly pared section. She carefully lifted a frosting flower from one side and used it and a couple of real flowers she skillfully pulled from the table decoration to cover the patched section.

"Now we'll just turn it a little, so this section is in the back," she said, gently spinning the cake a few inches then raised her hands. "And voila—good as new." She shrugged as she licked a small glob of icing from the side of her thumb. "Well, almost as good as new. And nobody has to know any different but us."

"You did it!" Mandy let out a whoop and threw her arms around Elizabeth's middle. "Thank you, Cousin Bitsy. You're the best."

Cousin Bitsy?

Ford had no idea what that meant, but they didn't have time for him to ask. "She's right. That *is* a work of art. You saved the day, but now we need to get out of here before they send a search party for us."

Mandy untied Shamus and headed for the door, calling over her shoulder, "Thanks again."

"You really did save the day," Ford told Elizabeth after they'd cleaned up the last remaining crumbs and tossed the bare cupcakes and the portion of the cake the horse's mouth had touched.

"It was nothing," she said, waving away his compliment.

"Don't do that. It *was* something," he told her, wrapping his arm around her waist and pulling her to him. "*You're* something. I think you're pretty incredible." He leaned down and brushed a soft kiss against her lips then spoke softly against her ear. "Elle would kill me if I did it now, but I'm looking forward to messing up that fancy lipstick of yours later tonight." He loved the shiver that raced through Elizabeth's shoulders and the little nervous giggle she let out. "But we gotta go now, or Elle and Brody will kill us both."

***

Other than the mini horse sampling the cake and Mandy's puppy, who was apparently the co-ringbearer, trying to eat the rose petals off the aisle-runner, the rest of the wedding went off without a hitch. Elle was gorgeous, and Brody got teary and choked up when he was reciting his vows which got most of the church to bawling as well.

Ford swore that half the town was in attendance as several hundred people filed into the barn after the ceremony and lined up at the buffet for pulled pork sandwiches and potato salad.

It felt like hours before he had another chance to talk to Elizabeth. She was either surrounded by family or the other bridesmaids, or helping to run food back and forth from the kitchen to the buffet line. Then he got roped into a cornhole tournament by another one of the groomsmen, which they lost, mainly because he couldn't keep his focus on the game due to him constantly trying to check out what Elizabeth was doing.

After the meal and the speeches and the cutting of the cake, the band began to play. Brody and Elle had *their* first dance then danced with their respective parents then finally invited everyone else to join in. Ford figured this was his best chance to get a few minutes alone with the woman who'd taken up way too many of his thoughts the last few days.

She was standing with Brody's mom and another woman, and Ford dipped his chin as he reached to cup Elizabeth's elbow. "Excuse me ladies, but can I steal this one for a dance?"

"Of course you can," Brody's mom said. "I'd never stand in the way of a handsome cowboy asking a girl to dance."

"Thanks, Mrs. T," he said, gently tugging Elizabeth toward the dance floor. "Congratulations on the wedding and all."

"Thanks Ford. Good to see you," she replied then called out to Elizabeth. "Have fun, Bitsy. He's one of the good ones."

"Nothing like getting the endorsement of your buddy's mom when you're trying to sweep a pretty woman off her feet." He pulled her into his arms as they joined the other couples on the dance floor.

"Is that what you're trying to do?" She peered up at him with a shy grin.

"Right now I'm just trying to keep from *stepping* on your feet," he said, grinning back as he fell into the slow, easy strides of the Texas Two-Step. He moved her around the dance floor, keeping one hand securely on her waist as he maneuvered around the other couples. "So why do all these folks keep calling you *Bitsy*?"

She cringed and shook her head. "It's just a stupid nickname."

He waited for her to say more.

"My parents tried to shorten Elizabeth to *Betsy*, but my little brother couldn't pronounce it and called me Bitsy instead. And unfortunately, it stuck. But I've never liked it."

"Why not? I think it's cute."

"Yeah, it is. A *cute* nickname. That's why I hate it." She gestured down at herself. "Look at me. I'm not someone that anyone would describe as cute or as a 'bitsy' little thing. I'm five-nine, and I've got curves for days. It just makes the whole thing sound ironic. And not in a good way."

He frowned at her. "I wish you wouldn't put yourself down. I love that you're tall. It makes it so I don't have to bend down so far to kiss you." He offered her a wolfish grin and slid his hand a little lower on her waist. "And I'm extremely fond of your curves and could spend *days* exploring them."

A grin tugged at the corner of her lips.

"And I *do* think it's cute because I think you're cute, but I'll keep calling you Elizabeth, since that's what you seem to prefer. Believe me, if anyone understands not being fond of their name, it's me."

"What? Why? I love the name Ford. It's hot."

Now it was his turn to grin. "I appreciate that. But you wouldn't think it's so hot if you met my brothers Dodge and Chevy."

She barked out a laugh, then covered her mouth with her hand as she tried to school her expression into something more solemn when he didn't laugh with her. "Oh. Goodness. You're serious?"

"Yep."

"Your brother's names are really Dodge and Chevy?"

He was used to this reaction. "Yep."

"Was your dad an auto mechanic? Or did he just love cars?"

"I wouldn't know. He split before I was born. My mom had three sons, all with different deadbeat dads, and she named each of us after the kind of truck our fathers drove away from us in."

"Oh. That's original, at least. And kind of cute, sort of," she said with a well-meaning shrug.

"Not really. My mom was an alcoholic, and she probably came up with the idea when she was drunk. Best thing she ever did for us boys was to dump us on the doorstep of our grandparents before she took off too. So, you can imagine why I'm not the greatest at relationships—having someone stick around for me isn't something I'm accustomed to."

Dang. Why did he tell her that? He *wasn't* good at relationships—hadn't ever been. Which was what Brody was referring to when he talked about why he was a good match for Elizabeth—she didn't sound like she was into relationships either. But there was something about this woman that maybe had him wanting to take a chance.

"My grandparents were great though," he told her. "They were the real deal. Got married at eighteen, and my grandpa was still crooning love songs to my gram in his eighties. They raised us on their ranch not too far from here, and we all went to school in Creedence. That's how I know Brody. And most of these people here. That's what happens when you grow up in a small town and go to a school with eighty-four people in your graduating class."

"I love that. My graduating class had six hundred people in it, and I probably still only see or talk to two of them. One, because she's my cousin, the other, because her family runs my favorite diner, and she still works there."

"Sounds kind of nice to me. Then at least half the town wouldn't always be in your business."

She shrugged and a quick look of sadness crossed her face. "The opposite of that is that *no one* cares what you do."

"I care," he said softly as he gazed down at her, that brief expression of sorrow touching his heart. It made him want to pick her up, carry her out of here, and never let anyone make her sad again. He liked her laugh and loved making her giggle or laugh so hard that she let out a snort.

She held his gaze, and her lips parted, just the slightest bit. He remembered how they felt against his, soft and supple, and he leaned closer, yearning to capture her mouth and taste her again.

The song ended before he could, and Elizabeth was called away by another bridesmaid. He leaned close to her ear before she slipped out of his arms. "I can wait around, after, in case you want a ride back to the cottage."

"I'd like that," she said, offering him a smile that held a promise of more to come, before she slipped away.

A hand grabbed his arm, and he turned to see Liz flashing him a flirty smile. It didn't faze him. He had an idea that she flashed that same smile to a lot of people.

"My turn for a dance," she said, leading him out onto the floor and pulling his arm around her. She leaned in close to his ear as he led her around the floor. "Thanks for introducing me to Liam. We've been having a great time. He took me back to his place last night and showed me his computer."

Ford grimaced as he looked down at her. "Gross. Is that code for...?"

She laughed. "No. He really *did* show me his computer. Then we watched Netflix and chilled." She lifted one shoulder and gave him a coy smile. "And that really *is* code for..."

He held up his hand. "Yeah, yeah. I get the picture."

She laughed again. "He's a sweet guy. Kind of like you."

"Me? Sweet is not something I usually get accused of."

"I saw you this morning, outside of the salon. I know you're the one who picked up the bagels for Bitsy."

He shrugged. "And?"

"*And*, I thought it was sweet. That's all. And it made me think maybe you were the one who she'd been 'camping' with the night before."

He shrugged again, not wanting to betray Betsy's confidence if she wanted their time together kept private.

"Bitsy is sweet, too," she told him, all traces of kidding gone as she took on a more serious expression.

"You don't have to tell me. I already know that."

"She's one of the good ones. So just be careful with her. Okay?"

"Okay," he said, his tone just as serious. He liked the fact that Liz was protecting her friend. He looked across the room and saw Elizabeth laughing as she doled out cupcakes to a table of kids who were all trying to pet Thor.

He was falling harder and harder for the pretty bridesmaid, and he had to wonder who was going to protect him when she left tomorrow.

Chapter Eleven

With so many people helping, it didn't take long to clean up after the reception was over. But to Ford, who couldn't stop thinking about kissing Elizabeth again, it seemed like it took forever.

"Can we get out of here now?" He leaned down and whispered to her as they stacked the last of the chairs against the wall.

She stifled a giggle, but her eyes shone with a sweet flirtation as she nodded. Tendrils of her hair had come loose from her up-do and lay across her bare neck, reminding him of the first time he saw her and how he'd wanted to touch them then. Now he wanted to pull all those bobby pins out and fill his hands with her silky curls.

The bride and groom had already left, so he headed outside to wait for Elizabeth as she said goodnight to her family and the other bridesmaids. He'd see most of these people again at the breakfast Brody and Elle had scheduled for the morning, so he wasn't concerned about telling anyone goodbye.

All his concerns were about getting Elizabeth back to her cottage and all the other parts of her he could fill his hands with.

He pushed away the thoughts that she was leaving in the morning and that she wasn't looking for anything other than a good time this weekend. They still had tonight, and he planned to make the best of it.

The cottage was only a short ten minute drive from Brody's ranch, and they spent the time making small talk about the wedding. She let Thor out when they got to the bed and breakfast, and he raced ahead of them to the cottage.

"Thanks for driving me back," Elizabeth said, when they reached her door. "You want to come in for a..." She paused and frowned up at him, and his nerves lurched at the thought that maybe she didn't want to invite him in. That maybe she wasn't really interested in hanging out with him anymore. "Oh shoot. I didn't think this through. I don't have anything to offer you. I don't have any alcohol in my room, or coffee, or even a pop. And the only snacks I have are dog treats and maybe a few mints rolling around the bottom of my purse." She raised her shoulders in a shrug. "Do you want to come in for some *water*?"

He chuckled. "As appealing as that purse mint and a dog treat sounded, I *do* still want to come in. And believe me, darlin', you have *plenty* to offer me. I've spent the whole day just thinking about when I could finally kiss you again."

Her eyes widened. "You have?"

"Hell yes, I have."

"Then it sounds like we've got some time to make up for, so you better get in here and start kissing me." She laughed as she unlocked the door and let Thor run into the room ahead of them. Tossing her bag onto the floor, she turned to him, and he swept her into his arms.

Her lips were just as soft and pliant as he'd remembered, and she tasted like wedding cake and champagne. He kicked the door shut behind them, then he turned her around and pressed her against it. His hands roamed over all her luscious curves as he kissed her lips, her neck, the bare skin of her shoulders.

Her fingers dug into his hair, pulling him close as she kissed his mouth with a hunger that matched his. He loved the soft kitten sighs she made as his lips trailed over her skin. He shrugged out of his jacket and wrenched the tie from his neck. Her fingers went to the buttons of his vest and shirt, fumbling in their haste to undo them quickly. He toed off his cowboy boots, and she reached to undo the clasp of her strappy heels.

"Wait," he said, taking her hand and pulling it above her head as he turned her to face the door. "Leave those on." His voice was husky against her ear as he used his free hand to draw the zipper of her dress down her back and his mouth to press hot kisses along her shoulders.

Another soft sigh then he released her hand, and she let her dress fall to the floor. She turned back to him, wearing the smile he'd dreamed about the night before.

A seductive smile that had his knees wanting to buckle. "You are so beautiful," he told her.

Her smile faltered, and she shook her head again, her shyness back. "No, I'm not."

"Yes, you are," he said, leading her toward the bed. "But if you don't believe me, I'll just have to spend the next few hours ravishing every single inch of your body, and confirming how amazing you are."

His words brought her flirty smile back, and he vowed to make good on his promise. Every. Single. Inch.

Elizabeth woke up the next morning the same way she had the day before, curled against the hot body of a naked cowboy who was palming her boob.

She could get used to this.

Although Ford *had* told her the night before that he wasn't the greatest at relationships. So, he didn't really seem like the type to stick around. But still—she really believed they had a connection.

She slipped out of bed and snuck in to use the bathroom and brush her teeth. When she came out, she was disappointed to see Ford was up and already had his pants and boots on.

He flashed her a grin as he pulled his shirt on that had her wishing she'd stayed in bed with him. "Mornin' Beautiful."

"Good morning. I was thinking I could run across to the B&B and grab us some coffee," she said, as if in explanation for why she'd slipped out of bed and put on a tank top and a pair of panties.

"That sounds great, but I can't stay. I need to run back to the ranch to get my chores done and take a shower so I can get back for Elle and Brody's send-off breakfast."

The couple had decided to hold a 'thank you' breakfast for the wedding party and close family before everyone left that afternoon and they went on their honeymoon.

She tried not to be disappointed that he was already leaving and offered him what she hoped was a flirty smile. "You can always shower here. We could save water *and* time if we do it together."

His lips curved into a wolfish smile. "Believe me, Darlin', if I started out this morning with you naked and wet in the shower, we'd never make it to the breakfast at all."

He made a valid point. And softened the blow of what felt like him quickly getting dressed and fleeing the scene of the crime.

"I almost forgot. I got something for you," he said, reaching for his jacket.

"Something for me? What do you mean?"

"It's nothing big," he said, shrugging off his thoughtfulness. "I was just at the Mercantile getting some medicine for Dixie yesterday, and I saw it on a display by the cash register. It made me think of you, so I just grabbed it."

She held up her hand. "Stop. You had me at *I was buying something for my sick dog and thought of you…*"

He chuckled and pulled a thin paper sack from his inside jacket pocket. "I meant to give it to you last night, but then we came in here, and I forgot pretty much everything else. I probably couldn't have even told you my name."

Curious, and touched by the fact that he'd bought her something because it made him think of her, she opened the bag and pulled out a silver necklace on a plastic placard. The necklace had a sterling silver chain and hanging from it was a small silver pendant of a shooting star. She gasped as she looked up at him. "Oh, Ford."

"It's not a real diamond," he said, referring to the glittering stone in the center of the star. "They don't carry a lot of fine jewelry down at the Mercantile. But I thought you might like it." He was teasing, but she knew he was trying to play off the sweetness of the gift.

"I *love* it. It's a perfect memory for this weekend."

"Yeah, I thought so too. I thought it might bring to mind that stuff we talked about the other night and remind you to go for the things you want and to just do one brave thing at a time. You know those meteors we saw were about the size of a pebble, but we could still see them shoot across the sky." He shrugged again and gazed down at the floor. "I don't know. I guess what I'm saying is that even small things can have a big result."

Elizabeth blinked at him and swallowed hard. Everything he was saying was hitting her like a lightning bolt to the chest. She threw her arms around his neck and hugged him, still clutching the necklace in her hand. "Thank you. This means a lot."

"I'm glad you like it. And I wish I could stay, but I gotta go. I'll meet you at the church in a bit for breakfast." He pressed a quick kiss to her lips then slipped out the door.

She spent the next hour taking her time getting ready, applying her makeup and styling her hair. She put on a light blue sundress and the shooting star necklace. For the first time in a long time, she felt good about herself, like she could take on the world.

Before this weekend, she'd never imagined she could get a guy like Ford Lassiter, but he'd spent not one, but the last *two* nights with her. And he hadn't been shy about showing his appreciation of her either.

But it was more than the way he'd ravished her body, and make no mistake, he had *ravished her* until she couldn't think straight, it was also the way he listened to her when she talked and asked questions about her life and seemed to want to know more about her. He made her laugh, and the funniest thing was that she seemed to make him laugh, too.

They'd spent the majority of the weekend together, so there hadn't been a need to exchange their contact information, but she hoped he'd ask for her number before they left the church breakfast.

She'd planned to drive back to Denver as soon as the breakfast was over, but maybe Ford would ask her to stay and spend the afternoon with him. Heck, she'd call in sick to work tomorrow if he wanted her to spend another night.

It took her a little longer than she thought it would to pack her things in the car and check out of the cottage, but she was still a few minutes early, and surprised to see Ford's truck already parked in front of the church.

She slipped through the front door and down the stairs, her footsteps hushed on the thick carpet. A small Sunday School room sat at the bottom of the stairs, and she almost walked past it as she headed for the doors leading into the main reception area of the basement. But she stopped when she heard Brody and Ford's voices and caught them talking about *her*.

She knew she shouldn't eavesdrop. She should just step into the room, or cough loudly, or go back up and come down the stairs again, but louder this time. But she didn't. She just stood outside the door and listened.

"Hey, I saw you dancing with my cousin last night," Brody had just said. "I told you she was great."

Ahhh. That was sweet. Love you too, Brody.

"I really appreciate everything you did for us this weekend," Brody continued.

"It was nothing," Ford said.

"I know we asked a lot of you. Filling in as my groomsman helped us out so much, but I also really appreciate the favor of you spending time with my cousin, too."

She jerked her head back then tried to swallow, but her mouth had gone dry.

Spending time with my cousin? What was he talking about? Had Ford only been hanging out with her as a *favor* to Brody?

"We had fun," Ford said.

"I knew you would. That's why we asked you to hang out with her. I told you she was just looking to have a good time this weekend, no strings attached. And Elle really nailed it. She knew you and Liz would hit it off."

Chapter Twelve

Elizabeth pressed her fingers to her lips and blinked back tears.

"Liz?" she heard Ford ask in a strange tone.

"Yeah, Liz. My cousin, Elizabeth," Brody said. "The one you were dancing with last night."

Liz? Brody had asked Ford to spend time with his cousin Elizabeth—and she'd taken Liz's nametag, so Ford had gotten stuck with the wrong one. She bet he'd be disappointed when he realized who he'd missed his chance to actually be with.

"No. You asked me to hang out with *Elizabeth*, the one with the cute little dog."

"Little dog?" Brody sounded confused. "Oh, you mean Bitsy?"

"Wait. You're telling me you and Elle were trying to set me up with *Liz*? Not Elizabeth? Or Bitsy?"

Hearing Brody, then Ford, say the nickname struck her chest like a knife to the heart. She backed slowly up the stairs.

She'd heard enough.

Ford thought he was doing Brody a *favor* by hanging out with his cousin, Elizabeth. He thought she was just looking for a good time this weekend. But he'd gotten stuck with the *wrong* Elizabeth.

Although with all her self-talk about being brave and having the courage to go for what she wanted, she'd practically thrown herself at the guy. And the way she'd behaved when they'd been together in the back of the truck, he wouldn't have known that was the first time she'd ever let herself act with such reckless abandon. She was sure, to him, it probably *had* seemed like she was just looking for a good time.

As soon as she reached the top step, she turned and fled from the church.

Ford couldn't believe what he was hearing. *Liz?* Not Elizabeth?

Dixie had been sitting by his side, and she suddenly stood and padded to the door.

"Yeah, I guess I can see now why you're confused," Brody said. "Technically, they are both named Elizabeth, but I assumed you knew I was talking about Liz. And we saw you dancing with her last night, so we thought you guys really hit it off."

He called Dixie back to his side. "We *did* hit it off…as friends. But I *really* hit it off with Elizabeth, I mean Bitsy, I guess. We had a great time hanging out this weekend."

"Huh? Who would've figured? You and Bitsy? Well, I'm glad for you then. Bitsy is a great girl."

Yeah, you would have really thought so if you'd seen her patching up your wedding cake after a mini horse took a bite out of it, Ford thought, as he and Brody carried the extra chairs they'd come in there for out to the reception area.

SAVE THE DATE FOR A COWBOY

The rest of the wedding party had started to arrive, and Ford looked around for Elizabeth. He thought she would've been here by now.

He checked his watch again ten minutes later, and another ten after that. He'd already finished eating and was working on a second cup of coffee, and she still wasn't there.

Maybe something had happened, and she needed help. Maybe her car hadn't started, or she'd tripped and sprained her ankle and was lying in the yard by the cottage just waiting for someone to find her.

And maybe he was being melodramatic. But something was off.

He might not know her *that* well, but after seeing how upset she was after being so late yesterday, there was no way she'd be late again today.

Something was wrong, and he needed to find her. He patted his leg for Dixie to follow and hurried up the stairs.

Elizabeth had run out of the church and back to the safety of her car. She'd set her bag on the seat next to her, and Thor must have sensed her distress because he climbed out of the bag and into her lap.

She hugged the little dog and tried not to cry as she replayed her cousin's words again in her head. She still couldn't believe it. He'd asked Ford to do him a *favor* and spend time with her. No, not *her*...her cousin, Liz. And Ford thought he was getting the party girl who was only looking for a good time.

She buried her face in her hands, embarrassed and humiliated. She felt like such a fool.

Although it kind of made sense now why Ford would be with her. It wasn't because of her kindness or even her sparkling wit. He was just looking to have a good time too.

But he'd bought her a necklace and told her she was beautiful. He'd said he'd prove it to her. And it felt like he had. Every kiss, every touch, every soft caress had made her believe she *was* beautiful.

And that belief was what had given her the courage to step out of her safe comfort zone.

She hugged Thor closer and thought about everything she'd done that weekend. She'd gone swimming in a lake and star-gazed with a hot cowboy. She'd roasted marshmallows and drank whiskey and had gone to O-Town under the stars in the back of a pickup, not *once* or even twice, but *four times*.

That was *definitely* stepping out of her box.

She'd danced and served cake and talked and laughed with other people beyond her own family. And she'd used her creativity and quick wit to repair the wedding cake fiasco.

She touched the shooting star pendant at her neck as she thought about the way she'd salvaged that cake. Maybe she needed to slice off the chewed-up parts of the weekend and slap some fresh frosting on it. She tried to think of another way to look at her time with Ford.

It *had* been an amazing weekend. And even if she was the wrong Elizabeth, they'd still had a great time together. She'd had mind-blowing sex with a ridiculously hot cowboy and done things she'd never imagined herself doing. But she'd still done them. And felt good about herself afterwards.

Maybe this weekend *hadn't* been a disaster. Maybe this weekend had been just what she needed.

Setting Thor on the passenger seat, she dug around the car looking for something to write on. An envelope from an old utility bill was the best she could come up with. It'd been on the floor and had a bit of a muddy paw print on one side, but it would have to do. She found a pen in her purse and scribbled a note to Ford before she lost her nerve.

Dear Ford,

I just overheard you talking to Brody in the church, and I know I wasn't what you thought you were getting this weekend—a fun girl looking for a good time. Don't worry I'm not mad. I was—at first. Not mad, really. More like sad. For you—that you ended up with the wrong bridesmaid. But I wanted to tell you that even though you were the fill-in for Brody, you were absolutely the right groomsman for me. I had the best weekend with you and spending that time together has made me believe that I do have the courage to make big changes in my life.

Even though you were only doing it as a favor to my cousin, spending time with you meant a lot to me. I know you said you weren't great at relationships and that's okay—because we'll probably never see each other again anyway—and that's not what I was looking for either. But I had the best weekend and will always remember the amazing time I spent hanging out in the mountains with a hot cowboy.

Thanks for showing me the stars... I think I'm finally ready to go out and shine like one.

Wishing you all the best,

Elizabeth

When she finished, she ran over to Ford's truck—no one locked their cars in this town—and left the note on his seat.

She couldn't face him. She wasn't that brave yet.

But she was getting there.

She was sad that she didn't get to say goodbye, but the note would have to do. Those parts about her not looking for a relationship and saying that was okay with her were the only parts of the note where she'd lied. In her heart, she'd already fallen for him. And when he gave her the necklace this morning, she'd thought for a second that maybe he was the one who might be her chance at finding her forever.

She let out a long breath as she got back in her car and started the engine. She *was* glad they'd had this weekend. Because sometime in the last few days, she'd changed. And now she was finally ready to take some risks and make some changes in her life.

She put the car in gear, but before she drove out of town and away from Ford, she made one last stop at the real estate agency.

Ford sat in his truck with Dixie's head resting on his leg and read the note one more time.

He'd known this was coming, known this weekend was too good to be true. He'd come to expect it, because this was what happened in his life—he wasn't the one worth sticking around for, he was the one who always got left behind.

So yeah, maybe for a minute, he'd wished things could have been different. Wished that they would have exchanged numbers at least. But maybe it was better this way. Clean break and all. And it was probably good she'd left him a note, because if she would have tried to say to him the things she'd written, he might have never let her go.

Damn. He still felt terrible that she'd overheard him and Brody talking. He replayed the conversation again in his head and hated to think anything he'd said had made her feel bad about herself.

This *had* been a perfect weekend, he thought as he carefully folded the note and tucked it inside his wallet. A weekend, *and a woman*, he would never forget.

But something told him she was going to be just fine. Not *just* fine—he saw amazing things ahead for her.

But if they ever crossed paths again, it sure would be hard for him not to want something more, and he imagined he would look back on this weekend and wonder if he'd missed his chance at finding the one who wouldn't have walked away.

The end...
...and just the beginning.

If you want to know what happens when Ford gets hired to help fix up the rundown farmhouse next-door to his ranch and realizes Elizabeth is the one who bought it...check out **Love at First Cowboy**: Book One in the **Lassiter Ranch** series. (Keep reading for a sneak peek at the first chapters...)

If you loved this small mountain town in Colorado, be sure to check out all the books in the hockey-playing **Cowboys of Creedence** series and the **Creedence Horse Rescue** series, where Elle and Brody first met. These stories are as heartbreaking as they are heartwarming and full of hot cowboys, smart heroines, and hilarious animal antics. The Heaven Can

Wait Horse rescue is a place where more than the animals find their forever homes.

"...swoon-worthy, must-read romance." —— Sara Richardson, National bestselling author

"Filled with humor, heart and real love." —— Michelle Major, *USA Today* bestselling author

Love At First Cowboy
Lassiter Ranch – Book 1
By Jennie Marts-
USA Today Bestselling Author

Chapter One

Ford Lassiter, and his brothers, Dodge and Chevy, had heard every joke in the book about their names. But the sad truth of it was that their Mama had named each of them after the truck that their individual deadbeat dads had driven away from them in.

Their mother had eventually abandoned them, too. But she'd driven off in a beat-up Honda Accord, after dropping them at their grandparents' ranch, then conveniently forgot to ever come back to pick them up again. Now he, *and* his brothers all drove the trucks of their namesakes, mostly to be contrary, but probably also a little to spite their Mama.

Ford drove a 1984 Seventh Generation F-series pickup that had belonged to his grandfather. It had been his first truck, a gift from his grandparents when he'd turned sixteen. He'd had it repainted navy blue and had rebuilt the engine twice. And she still purred like a kitten as he drove under the bare-timber arched *Lassiter Ranch* sign and pulled out onto the highway.

He didn't have far to go. Not that *anywhere* in the small Colorado mountain town of Woodland Hills was far to go, but this trip was only taking him to the neighboring ranch.

Still can't believe someone actually bought this place, he thought as he turned down the driveway and eyed the old farm.

He remembered Frank and Ida Johnson—the older couple who'd lived there for as long as he could remember. They'd been not just neighbors, but friends of his grandparents. Ida had occasionally watched them after school, and he and his brothers had helped bring in their hay every summer. Ida made the best oatmeal butterscotch cookies he'd ever tasted.

The house had been deserted for the last several years, and it hurt his heart a little to see how much it had fallen into disrepair. As Frank and Ida had aged, so had the house, and Frank hadn't been able to keep up with all the repairs, like fixing the porch or covering the wood siding with fresh paint. Ford hadn't been here in a year or so, but as he parked in front of the house, he could still remember the way it had looked when he was younger, and the place brought back good memories.

The once-cheery yellow two-story Victorian farmhouse had faded to almost white, and the sagging front porch, with its rotted wood and multiple holes, looked like a strong gust of wind could blow the whole dang thing right off. Most of the windows were cracked or broken, a few replaced with plywood, and the gutters hung loose on one side and were completely missing on the other. The wood looked to be rotted clear through on the steps leading up to the porch, and one of the banisters had plum fallen off and lay in the dirt next to the steps.

It had once had the charm of a quaint gingerbread house, with elaborate decorative corbels under the corniced roofline, dormer windows, and one corner of the house extending out in a round turret that went all the way up to an attic room at the top.

The small front yard, once full of flower gardens, was overrun with weeds, and the previously bright white picket fence had faded to a dull gray and leaned precariously close to the ground. Thankfully, the barn still stood strong. It was newer than the house, and just needed a fresh coat of paint to return it to its former glory.

He felt sorry for the new owner. This place looked like a big old money pit now. But all those repairs meant cash in the bank to him. Fall harvest was just around the corner, and one of their combine implements had just broken. It was going to cost a few thousand dollars to purchase a new one, so Ford had been downright grateful when the local real estate agent had called and asked if he'd be interested in a side gig to help renovate this place. The new owner had bought it sight unseen, and they were looking to hire someone with construction experience to help with the repairs and to fix it up.

Ford and his brothers had been working on their grandparents' ranch since they were kids. Duke, their granddad, had taught them everything from how to rope a steer to how to wield a chainsaw. They'd even spent a summer helping to renovate the hunting cabin in the mountains behind the ranch, adding a bedroom, a bathroom, and updating the kitchen with running water and appliances. Ford enjoyed working with his hands and watching a project come together. That summer, he'd learned everything construction-related, from floor joists to roof trusses, from plumbing to electrical.

And this house looked like it would need them all.

Thinking about the hunting cabin brought up memories of the amazing night he'd spent there earlier that summer with a woman who'd acted like she cared about him then left him behind.

His brothers razzed him about being a grump and spending too much time reading, or hanging out with his dog or his horse, and their razzing probably had some merit. He *was* a bit of a grouch, but that weekend, the one he'd spent with Elizabeth Cole, had been the most fun he'd had in years. And not just the time they'd spent in her bed *and* in the bed of his pickup—although he'd spent many nights since reliving those times—it was more than that. She'd made him laugh, and he'd talked more to her in that one night at the cabin, sitting in front of the fire and watching the meteor shower, than he had to anyone else in years.

A grin tugged at the corner of his lips thinking about that campfire and the sight of her bikini underwear going up in flames.

But it hadn't mattered how much fun they'd had, or the connection that he'd thought they felt.

She'd left anyway.

He couldn't blame her. Not after she'd overheard the conversation he'd had with the groom about how he didn't do relationships, and that he was supposed to have spent that weekend of the wedding hooking up with the *other* bridesmaid named Elizabeth instead of her.

At least she'd left a note. He'd read the thing so many times the edges were worn, and the envelope she'd written it on was bent from being tucked into his wallet for the last month.

It wasn't the first time he'd been dumped. He'd learned it was easier to be the first one to walk away—hurt less that way. But he'd felt something with Elizabeth, something different, something that made him think he might have a chance at that elusive happiness...and maybe even love. He'd sure thought he was falling at the time.

He stepped from the truck then held the door open for Dixie, his golden retriever, to jump out. She ran to the car in the driveway to sniff the tires, and he noted with a jolt that the compact white SUV was the same kind Elizabeth drove.

His chest tightened as his gaze jumped to the door of the house.

Could Elizabeth be here?

No way. What the hell would she be doing at the ranch next to his? She did have cousins all over the county. Maybe one of them had bought this farm.

Or maybe this car was just one of the million compact white SUV's out there, and he was just manifesting Elizabeth being here because she was on his mind. *Like usual.*

Dixie let out a bark and ran through the yard and up the rickety porch steps. The inside door was open, and the outer wooden screen door banged against the jamb as if being bumped against from the other side. A small yip came from inside the house then the screen door opened just enough for a small orange and white dog to squeeze through.

An orange and white dog that Ford recognized.

Thor.

There was no mistaking the dog. Elizabeth had told him it was a Havanese, and he'd never seen another one like it. And if there was any question that it was Elizabeth's dog, it would be squashed by the way the two dogs were racing around the yard together, tumbling over each other with excitement and recognition.

"Thor! Get back here!" a voice called from inside. A voice Ford had been hearing in his dreams. Obviously not the voice she was using to holler for the dog, but he knew it as well as he knew his own heart.

As if by their own volition, his feet started walking toward the house.

The screen door banged open. And then she was there—standing on the porch in a short white sun dress and high-heeled cowboy boots, her hair a mess of chestnut curls around her shoulders.

"Elizabeth," he breathed her name.

She froze, staring at him as if he were a mirage.

"Ford?" She took a step forward, her expression a mix of surprise and astonishment. "What are you doing he—?" she started to say as she took a step toward him.

Then a loud crack sounded as the old boards gave way, and she fell through the floor of the porch.

Chapter Two

Elizabeth Cole, affectionately known as Bitsy to her family, felt anything but 'bitsy' as her tall, curvy body crashed through the rotted floorboards of her new front porch.

There was close to a five-foot drop, and she cried out as first her knee then her hip then her forehead hit the jagged boards as she fell into the dark space. Her legs crumpled under her, and she shrieked at the feel of whispery legs skittering across her shins.

"Hold on," Ford called.

She could hear his bootheels racing across the sidewalk and up the steps. How in the heck was Ford Lassiter standing in her front yard? She hadn't seen the handsome cowboy since the morning she'd left a note and driven away from him and the small town of Creedence, where she'd been severely humiliated and had also had undoubtably the best, *and hottest*, weekend of her life.

The humiliation came from the fact that Ford had spent the weekend with *her* by mistake. He was meant to be set up with her gorgeous, and much more fun, cousin—also named Elizabeth. But the weekend they'd shared together had been glorious. The time she'd spent with Ford and the way she'd stepped out of her comfort zone to be with him is what had given her the courage to make some huge changes in her life. Including buying this place.

This place that was literally falling down around her ears.

She waved her hands at the sticky spider webs trying to clutch at her clothes and hair and screamed as another creepy crawly skittered across her arm. The space under the porch was dark and damp, full of dead leaves and old boards.

Ford's strong hands reached down for her. His voice held a note of panic as he clasped her arms. "Are you okay? Are you hurt? Can you stand up?"

Stunned and hurt, she was trying to get her bearings as she struggled not to cry. Like, *really* struggled.

She swallowed around the huge lump in her throat. "I'm okay," she said, trying to keep her voice from wobbling. "I'm just embarrassed." She tried to get her feet under her. "And my knee hurts and my head hurts. And I think I scraped my arm." She didn't know what hurt more—the aches in her body, or her pride. Her voice rose as she slapped at her legs. "Holy crap! It feels like there's bugs crawling all over me."

"It's okay. I got you." Ford got a hold of her under her arms and hauled her up and out of the hole. She scrambled to gain purchase with her feet but leaned into him as he pulled her up. She hadn't seen him in weeks—was, in fact, a little mad at him—no, that didn't make sense, but she'd think about that later. Right now, she was grateful for his strength and clung to his shoulders.

"Let's get you inside and assess the damage," Ford said, keeping his arm around her and carefully avoiding another hole in the porch boards as he opened the screen door and led her inside.

She'd bought the house 'as-is' which basically meant that she was stuck fixing everything and that no one had come in to remove all the discarded furniture. A small, ragged settee—that she already had big plans to re-cover—and an old farmhouse table with two mismatched chairs sat in the living area, and Ford led her to one of the chairs.

Sinking into it, she finally peered down at her legs to assess the damage…and saw an earwig stuck to her knee. At the same time, she felt something whispery on her arm and looked down to see a spider skittering across her forearm. And another one on the front of her dress. And another on her chest.

"Gah! Get them off me!" She pushed out of the chair and started limp-hopping around as she slapped at her arms and legs and the front of her dress. "Spiders! I hate spiders!" She couldn't see them, but she could feel them, and was sure they were in her clothes.

Her formerly white dress was covered in dirt and blood and something that looked like rust. And *so* many spiderwebs. She shrieked again as she saw a bug of some kind drop into her boot.

She had to get out of these clothes.

She didn't even think. She just grabbed the hem of her dress, hauled it over her head, and flung it on the floor. Hopping on one foot, she tried to get her boot off, but the damn thing was too tight. Why had she let that salesgirl talk her into these stupid boots anyway?

"Help me!" she cried to Ford. "There's a spider in my boot." Stars spun around her head as she bent forward, and a drop of blood hit the floor in front of her. She reached up to press her fingers to her throbbing head, but her forehead was damp and sticky.

Oh no. She didn't do well with blood. *Please don't be blood.*

She pulled her fingers away, and the room swam around her as she saw the bright red blood covering them. Her knees buckled and gave way under her.

From far away, she heard the sound of Ford's curse, then everything went black.

To find out what happens next, grab ***Love at First Cowboy***: Book One in the ***Lassiter Ranch*** series.

SAVE THE DATE FOR A COWBOY

ALSO BY JENNIE MARTS

Thanks for reading SAVE THE DATE FOR A COWBOY!
If you enjoyed this book, I'd love to invite you to check out my other titles, ranging from hockey-playing cowboys to cozy mysteries:

LASSITER RANCH
Save the Date For a Cowboy

Love at First Cowboy

Overdue for a Cowboy

COWBOYS OF CREEDENCE
Caught Up in a Cowboy

You Had Me at Cowboy

It Started with a Cowboy

Wish Upon a Cowboy

CREEDENCE HORSE RESCUE
A Cowboy State of Mind

When a Cowboy Loves a Woman

SAVE THE DATE FOR A COWBOY

How to Cowboy

Never Enough Cowboy

Every Bit a Cowboy

A Cowboy Country Christmas

THE PAGE TURNERS COZY MYSTERY/ROM COMS

Another Saturday Night and I Ain't Got No Body

Easy Like Sunday Mourning

Just Another Maniac Monday

Tangled Up in Tuesday

What To Do About Wednesday

A Cowboy For Christmas: A Page Turners Holiday Novella

A Halloween Hookup: A Page Turners Holiday Novella

BEEKEEPING COZY MYSTERIES

Take the Honey and Run

Kill or Bee Killed

THE BANNISTER BROTHERS: HOCKEY ROMANCE/ROM COMS

Worth the Shot

Icing on the Date

Skirting the Ice

HEARTS OF MONTANA: WESTERN ROMANCE

Tucked Away

Hidden Away

Stolen Away

COTTON CREEK ROMANTIC COMEDY SERIES

Romancing the Ranger

Hooked on Love

Catching the Cowgirl

JENNIE MARTS

NOVELLAS
How to Unbreak a Heart
Melted

About the Author

Jennie Marts is the *USA TODAY* Best-selling author of award-winning books filled with love, laughter, and always a happily ever after. Readers call her books "laugh out loud" funny and the "perfect mix of romance, humor, and steam." Fic Central claimed one of her books was "the most fun I've had reading in years."

She is living her own happily ever after in the mountains of Colorado with her husband, two dogs, and a parakeet who loves to tweet to the oldies. She's addicted to Diet Coke, adores Cheetos, and believes you can't have too many books, shoes, or friends.

Her books range from western romance to cozy mysteries but they all have the charm and appeal of quirky small town life. She loves genre-mashups like adding romance to her Page Turners cozy mysteries and creating the hockey-playing cowboys in the Cowboys of Creedence. The same small-town community comes to life with more animal antics in her latest Creedence Horse Rescue series. And her sassy heroines and hunky heroes carry over in her heartwarming, feel good romances from Hallmark Publishing.

Jennie loves to hear from readers. Follow her on Facebook at *Jennie Marts Books*, Twitter at *@JennieMarts,* and/or Instagram at *jenniemartswriter*. Visit her at jenniemarts.com and sign up for her newsletter to keep up with the latest news and releases.

SAVE THE DATE FOR A COWBOY

Printed in Great Britain
by Amazon